D0362688

WANDER

WANDER

Lori Tobias

Wander
Copyright © 2016 by Lori Tobias
All Rights Reserved

No part of this book may be used or reproduced in any manner whatsoever without the prior written permission of both the publisher and the copyright owner.

Book design and layout by Cierra Coppini

Library of Congress Cataloging-in-Publication Data
Names: Tobias, Lori, author.
Title: Wander / Lori Tobias.
Description: First edition. | Pasadena, CA : Boreal, 2016.
Identifiers: LCCN 2016023205 (print) | LCCN 2016031727 (ebook)
    | ISBN 9781597099899 (paperback) | ISBN 9781597099639
Subjects: LCSH: Wives—Fiction. | Radio journalists—Fiction. | Man-woman
relationships—Fiction. | Loss (Psychology)—Fiction. | Alaska—Fiction. | Psychological fiction. | BISAC: FICTION / General. | GSAFD: Mystery fiction.
Classification: LCC PS3620.O246 W36 2016 (print) | LCC PS3620.
    O246 (ebook) | DDC 813/.6—dc23
LC record available at https://lccn.loc.gov/2016023205

The Los Angeles County Arts Commission, the National Endowment for the Arts, the Pasadena Arts & Culture Commission and the City of Pasadena Cultural Affairs Division, the Los Angeles Department of Cultural Affairs, Dwight Stuart Youth Fund, Sony Pictures Entertainment, and the Ahmanson Foundation partially support Red Hen Press.

First Edition
Published by Boreal Books
an imprint of Red Hen Press, Pasadena CA
www.borealbooks.org
www.redhen.org

ACKNOWLEDGMENTS

Throughout my career as a writer, I have been blessed with the best friends and teachers, and I am grateful to every one of them.

I want to especially express my sincere thanks to Sandra Scofield for taking me under her wing way back when I was just getting started, and to the Squaw Valley Community of Writers for welcoming me into their fold and truly opening a community to me. To Literary Arts for an Oregon Literary Fellowship and all that lovely time at Caldera. And finally, to Lucia, Lisa, Victoria, Mary, and Mark, who were always there to read, to listen, to laugh and commiserate, and who never failed to give me a lift when my spirits were low.

In memory of my mom, who instilled in me a love of words, and my dad, always with a story to tell.

And dedicated to Chan, the one person who knows me inside and out . . . and loves me anyway. Or to borrow a line from a certain fictional character, "I can't say if there is such a thing as soul mates, but I can say that finding Chan was like finding home."

WANDER

ONE

Once, when I was a young wife, I fell in love. He was like no one I'd known. He came from money. He went to Harvard. He wore perfect white shirts and murmured poetry in a voice that made every sentence sound like a song. He loved Paris and good Scotch.

And he wanted to die.

I didn't know that then. I was too busy chasing my own dreams. We all were.

In our little village of Wrassell, in the middle of nowhere, Alaska, we saw all kinds of prizes beckoning on the horizon, and we couldn't wait to get there. What we couldn't know was that it was not those glittering tomorrows that mattered, but those days right then and there. Because, as it turned out, they would be the last of their kind.

By the time that winter was over, three of us would be dead, another forever lost, and all of us changed, knowing that the days ahead, whatever they were to be, would shine just a little less brightly.

I was one of the lucky ones. I survived, and still with a wish to live, though not without the lesson of some hard truths. About love, for one, that as grand as it may be, it is also wildly imperfect. And about the heart, that it is a fickle compass, ready to mislead at a wink. Also, about pain, that, yes, it is possible to feel your heart break, and yes, you can pick up the pieces and put it back together again, but the cracks will still be there, and you will always, always know it.

It all began on the day in January when my husband, Nate, persuaded me he should go away. It was supposed to be a good thing.

KWLD was the new big deal on Bidarkee Bay. All oldies, all the time. I was the news director. We operated out of a two-story wood house on a street renamed just for us: Melody Lane. The downstairs was mostly storage; our offices took up the second floor.

I was in the newsroom getting ready to go on the air when my headphones crackled with static, then went dead. I ran to the file cabinet out front where we tossed the misfit headsets and grabbed a pair.

"Excuse me, Miss?"

He was a thin man: average height, round, gold wire-rimmed glasses, trench coat, fedora—no local, this guy.

"Yes?" I said.

Jeremy rapped on the glass from his studio, then tapped a finger against his wrist in the place where a watch would be were he wearing one, and punched up my intro music. In seconds it would end, leaving only dead air.

"Shit," I yelled. Jeremy, you prick. Jeremy was our new big star morning drive jock, all the way from somewhere in the Lower 48. Jeremy was going to show us how radio was done.

I left the stranger standing there looking mildly surprised and raced to the newsroom. I dropped into the chair, pulled on the headset, and rolled up to the mic. "Good morning, you're listening to a KWLD news update. I'm Pete Nash and it's eleven o'clock. KWLD temperature is . . ." I leaned back in my chair and searched in vain through the frosted window for a glimpse of the thermometer, then bluffed, "seventeen degrees."

I led the newscast with the story of a former state senator who got nailed for a DUI, then punched up the tape from my phoner with the senator that morning, and finally caught my breath as the tape played. *"Just a nip and tuck of cough medicine I keep in the truck . . . No harm there. The police these days, why between them and those MADD women, a man daresn't even treat a cold . . ."*

The tape ended. I wrapped up the newscast—oil prices plunge, Rock Hudson rumored to be infected with scary new disease AIDS, more trouble with Gaddafi, sports—and signed off.

Denny poked his head inside the door. "Good job on the senator," he said. "I can't believe the old goat actually said that. You call it into the AN?"

I held up the slip of paper torn from the wire with the story, my name, and our call letters at the top.

AN was shorthand for the Alaska News Network. You called in a breaking story and they sent it out to media outlets all over the state. Every month, they gave out prizes for the most stories and best story, and I was desperate to win both.

"Good job," Denny said. "Hey, by the way, there's someone I want you to meet." He pushed the door open wider and I saw then he wasn't alone.

"Pete, I'd like you to meet Reynolds Kennedy. Actually, that's Reynolds Kennedy III," Denny added in that teasing way he had.

"Ren's fine," he said with a shy smile, exposing perfect white teeth and crinkling olive-hued cheeks in dimples that radiated all the way up to what I noticed now were really very pretty blue eyes. Minus the trench coat, he was even slighter, and the missing fedora revealed a mostly bald scalp.

"Ren," Denny said, "this is Pete, our news director."

"Nice to meet you, Pete," he said, reaching for my hand.

"Ren's new to town," Denny said. "He did some radio back in his college days. Harvard," he added, raising his brows for emphasis. "I'm going to talk him into helping us out from time to time."

"Cool," I said.

"Yep, and you know the old Borealis Inn?"

"I think so."

"Well, this is the guy. Belonged to his family and now Ren's going to get it fixed up and opened again."

He turned to Ren to see if he might want to add something, but Ren just stood looking mildly embarrassed.

"Can you imagine doing a live broadcast from the old place, maybe even hosting a small dance. We'll knock their socks off. Oh, and speaking of . . ."

I listened as he went over, for the ninety-ninth time, everything he expected from us for the sock hop we would be hosting. Denny was on top of the world those days. Everything ahead was golden. Sometimes even I wondered if he was delusional.

"Got it?" he asked, finishing.

"Got it."

"Good, then we'll let you get back to work."

"Nice meeting you, Ren," I said.

Ren gave a small wave, and Denny pulled the door behind them, then just as quickly ducked back in. "Almost forgot, your sports news, it's Rose. Rosé's the wine. But at least you got the first name right."

He shut the door again. I felt my cheeks warm. Rose. Who the hell knew these things?

The newsroom line lit up red, reminding me that I needed to make my morning call to the cops to see if anything was going on. I tried to call twice each morning. Once at the start and again before I signed off. Usually, there was nothing, at least nothing big, but in a small town like this, you took what you could get, and you ignored what appeared to be the small stuff at your own peril, as I would learn the hard way.

I pulled on the headset and clicked the switch on the soundboard to phone.

"KWLD newsroom," I answered, using the mic to talk through the phone.

"Hey, Babe."

"Nate. Where are you?"

"Fueling up. I should be back at the hangar in a couple of hours."

"Everything OK?" I asked.

"Everything's great. I was just calling to say I love you and see how your day is going."

"My day's going great, and I love you, too. But I was just about to make my last cops call, so I can pull my noon news together."

"Pete, wait," he said. That's when I knew that whatever it was that had inspired the call, it was not just to say those three little words and how're you doing? Nate rarely called me by name. It was always Blondie or Babe or whatever else rolled off his tongue at the moment.

"Nate? What?"

"Well, what would you say if I told you I have an offer to go to work on the slope?"

"The slope? Nate, are you serious?"

"It would be temporary."

"So would our marriage," I joked.

"Just think about it, Babe. OK?"

"Nate? Really?"

"We'll talk when I get home."

We said our usual I love yous and hung up.

I did my noon news that day with no idea what I was reading, because while listeners may have heard me broadcasting live from Melody Lane, I was far, far away, thinking about all the money there was to be made "on the slope," that near-legendary place way the hell up there with all that oil just waiting to be drilled. But it was no nine-to-five, Monday-through-Friday job. Men went to the slope and stayed. And back home their wives drove new cars and sported good furs and gold nugget jewelry.

And here we were so broke. Even living cheap, we'd blown through the savings from Nate's summer guiding and our permanent dividend checks twice as fast as we'd expected. The paycheck I brought home was barely enough to feed us. Nate was no lazy guy. He'd chop firewood, plow snow, fly anywhere. But this year, the snow had been stubbornly spare, and bush pilots were not in demand. It was the eighties and things were tough all over.

I was beginning to fear this was the way it would always be, always struggling just to make ends meet. I was beginning to fear that one day we would awake to find ourselves middle-aged and still living in our little cabin, no phone, wood fire, still driving rusted old cars. Dreams long gone. There wasn't much in the world that scared me, but that left me cold.

By the time I got to the weather and my sign-off, I knew there was no way in hell I could say no.

That afternoon, I unplugged the Scout from the electrical socket that kept the engine from freezing and headed for home. At 4:30, it was dark as night, and I drove ever weary of the black ice that had already sent me flying once that winter and the moose that tended to pop out of the woods and plant themselves in the glow of your headlights.

Fifteen miles up the highway, I turned onto the snow-packed lane carved through a forest of tall, skinny spruce and pine, then down the small slope to the frozen Lasso Lake. By land, home was two-and-a-half miles of road so rutted and bumpy that your kidneys hurt; by lake it was one mile of mostly smooth ice. Some lakes got so busy they put up traffic signs: Stop. Yield. 25 mph. Lasso Lake was long and empty and lonely, with only the dim light from an occasional house tucked deep into the woods to say you weren't the sole inhabitant on the earth.

It took me five minutes to cross the lake then drive up over the sloped bank and onto the gravel road and home.

Smoke drifted from the cabin chimney. I ran a hand through my hair to tame the curls that got unruly by the end of the day and met my own dark gaze in the mirror. The slope. I couldn't even imagine. What would I do all winter alone? What wouldn't I do for that kind of paycheck.

I heard the thwack and followed the sound to the woodpile where a couple of camp lanterns lit up the night. Nate was splitting wood—his muscles working beneath the red cotton top of his union suit, his legs planted solid in faded jeans, frayed edges brushing the tips of his leather work boots, freshly oiled and newly laced. There was the shadow of whiskers that always darkened his jaw by late afternoon, and his dark hair curled from beneath the wool cap he pulled over his ears.

Nate was one of those Alaska-born guys, naturally at home in the natural world. He knew things, like how to find his way around the woods, build a fire with next to nothing, or make a snow cave or witch a well for water. He didn't scare easily, stayed calm when everyone else was falling apart, and didn't much care what other people thought—which meant sometimes you had to remind him that his jeans were dirty or shirt torn or that his razor sorely needed a new blade. And I was mad about him. Absolutely attached at the hip. I can't say if there is such a thing as soul mates, but I can say that finding Nate was like finding home.

He tossed the wood onto the pile and reached for another log, then seeing me, planted the ax in the tree trunk.

We met on the little porch by the door.

"The slope?" I said.

"Not even a kiss hello?"

I stood on tiptoe and kissed him.

"There, now tell me."

And so he did, about the oil exec who regularly hired him to fly him out to check on his fishing cabin, about the construction project and his offer to Nate to take a foreman's job, all the hours he could work. It was perfect. He'd be back just in time to get his boat on the water and guide again.

"But Nate, that's nearly five months from now. You couldn't come home at all?" By then, I'd been in Wrassell little more than a year, and that was adjustment enough for a girl who grew up in a city where the biggest patch of green was the local cemetery.

"Oh, I'm sure I'll be able to get away if I need to, but this job's on a deadline. The whole idea is to get 'er done, make money for the company, make money for us. If we're going to do that, I'll need to work all the hours I can. That's the only reason I'm going."

"Hell, Nate, I barely know how to build a fire."

"You build a fine fire, Babe" he said.

"I am fifteen miles from town and we have no phone. What if I get snowed in?"

"Honey," he said, twisting the cap off a bottle of Bud. "You know how to use a shovel, and there's the snowmobile if you really had to."

I tapped a glass of white zin from the box in the fridge.

"If you want me to turn it down, I will," he said.

"But I know you, you've already said yes."

"I can tell them I changed my mind."

"You would never forgive me."

"Of course I would," he said. "Besides, there would be nothing to forgive."

But that wasn't true. This was our chance, and we both knew it. This was the boost we needed to dig ourselves out of just getting by. This was where we got serious about putting the money away for Nate's own plane. And after that, a second boat. Then, a bigger plane, and one day, winters in Hawaii. Weekends in the city. The big old house with a fireplace in the kitchen and a hot tub on the deck, and a runway right out front where I could wave him in and see him off. That was our dream.

Nate had grown up under the care of his grandparents, simple country people, after his parents had disappeared in the floodwaters of the tsunami of '64. I was raised in a New Jersey row house by the railroad tracks in a family that lived paycheck to paycheck, lottery ticket to lottery ticket, ever hopeful those six lucky numbers would lead to the land of plenty. I wanted more, as much as I could get.

"Go," I said.

"Pete?"

"I'm serious. When do you have to leave?"

"Monday."

"Monday?" I said and felt my stomach flip. "That soon?"

Nate and I met at Fur Rendezvous, ten days of dog sled races, snow-shoe softball, downhill canoeing, carny rides, ice sculptures, and, that day, the grand prix.

I was between shifts at the hotel restaurant where I waited tables to pay my way through school. The sidewalks were solid with people watching the Karmann Ghias, Audis, and Fiats tear down the snow-packed streets. With the windchill factor, the temperature must have been minus fifteen, and I was thinking I must be some kind of idiot standing out there, toes like popsicles, face cold enough to crack.

"Hey, Blondie," I heard someone call from behind.

And even though there must have been five dozen blondes packed in that crowded block, I knew that voice was calling me. They say there are seven men for every woman in Alaska, but that didn't mean any one of those seven was anyone you'd want to meet. In Alaska you could meet the nicest guy in the crappiest bar and the crappiest guy in the best place in town. The man on the street who looked like a bum could as easily be a millionaire, and the guy dressed like a million was probably dealing coke.

"Hello?" came the voice again.

I turned and there was Nate, dark curly hair and dark eyes. The checkmark scar beneath his left eye, the result, I would learn, of an errant fishhook. He was lean, his skin already bearing the vague weathering of a man comfortable outdoors, and I could tell even then that this was a guy who was one part cocky, one part shy. And damn, he was good looking. He jumped from the cab of the big yellow grader.

"There's room for one more up there if you want to join me, he said, nodding toward the Caterpillar parked by the side of the road, one of several they'd used to make the race track. "Best view in the house."

"Me? Up there?"

"It's warm." He jammed his hands in his pockets. "Shame to waste a front row seat."

I laughed and he got embarrassed, and in that moment we weren't nearly the strangers we'd been.

That night he met me outside the hotel at the end of my shift. Right off, he took my hand, kissed me like we'd been doing it awhile, then said, "Heels? You'll break your neck."

"I can't dance in flats," I said.

His grin grew wider. "We're going dancing?"

"We don't have to."

"We can do anything you like."

We married six months later at a log cabin church with a view of the inlet.

I wore an ivory velvet gown that I found at a going-out-of-business sale in a downtown boutique. Nate wore a black tux borrowed from a pilot friend, and even with the brown dress shoes that should have been black, he looked like he walked straight out of a tuxedo ad in *Bride* magazine. We read vows we wrote ourselves, exchanged simple gold bands—just until we could afford something better—and when the preacher, a mustached Methodist who wore mukluks beneath his robe, pronounced me Patrice Nash, I thought I must be the luckiest girl in the world.

The next spring we moved to Wrassell, where Nate owned five acres an old miner had traded him for his pilot services. Wrassell was on Bidarkee Bay, both a body of water and the name of an area the size of a small state with not twenty thousand people.

I had no idea how I, a city girl to the core, was going to manage in so much wildness, but I would have followed Nate anywhere.

That weekend, a chinook blew in, driving the temperature to a balmy thirty-five and making the world seem just a little less unfriendly. We took care of all those things I didn't even know need-ed taking care of with Nate issuing endless reminders for my safety.

"Make sure you keep the Scout plugged in. You won't have the pickup. I said I'd leave it at the hangar so they can plow. And watch the potholes on the road this spring. You hit one of those right and you'll break an axle and that will be the end of the Scout. Take the lake as long as you can."

"Even when it's warm like this?" I asked.

"Of course. It's Alaska, Pete. That ice will be good 'til March, at least."

Then, too soon, it was Sunday afternoon, the wood was stacked, the chimney cleaned, his bags packed.

He led me outside and handed me the .38. "Don't use this un-less you have to, but if you have to, don't hesitate. And if you get in serious trouble, like, say a bear, you've got the shotgun. Under-stand?"

I nodded. Shit. Bears.

"All right, let's see you hit the bull's-eye," Nate said.

I fired off a round at the orange target. The first shots were way off, some missing the barrel.

Nate gave me that look: Come on, you can do better than that.

I took a couple of breaths and made myself quiet, lifted the gun to shoulder level, sent my eye down the length of the barrel, zeroed in on the target, and shot. Closer. I sighted it in again and watched a hole burst open one circle from the bull's-eye. The rest fell some-where near.

Nate squeezed my shoulder. "That's how you do it, Babe. Don't mess around."

"Nate, I know. I'll be fine," I said.

"I know you will, or I wouldn't be going."

He rested his hand on the small of my back, kissed the top of my head.

"I'm going to miss you, Pete," he said.

"Me too," and with no warning at all, my eyes filled.

He turned me around to face him, clucked my chin. "Come on now, don't you start or you'll get me started."

He pulled out his handkerchief—folded neat in a square—from his pocket, dabbed at my eyes. "Here," he said, holding it to my nose, "blow."

That night when we climbed into the loft, we made love long and slow and carefully, as if by taking our time, we might remember enough to last us.

TWO

One week after I watched Nate's plane nose high into the sky, KWLD hosted its first sock hop. We held it at the Russian Orthodox community hall, a cavernous old wood building with scarred floors and a massive stone fireplace we were forbidden to light. Next to it sat the cemetery, a rectangle of graves marked by little wood houses, each topped by a cross. I'd once watched a son dig his father's grave at a funeral there. I barely knew the deceased, a pilot friend of Nate's, but seeing that kid, head bent, dirt flying, I understood sorrow like my own language. Now, the memory fit my mood. I didn't just miss Nate; I mourned him.

I searched for a good plug-in for the Scout, but they were all taken or busted. The temperatures had been fairly mild, rising a couple of degrees above freezing by day, so I figured it would be OK for a bit. Better, it was one more excuse to get out of there early. I was in no mood for sixties love songs.

I hung my parka in the little front room with everyone else's and swapped my moon boots for black patent leather high heels.

Inside, Denny and Di led a crowded room in the twist.

"So screw you, too, don't say hello," I heard from behind me.

I turned and found Kate Brady, news director at our rival station, KBAY. A petite woman with a blonde bob and only the slightest hint of makeup, she wore the usual: black cardigan, black slacks, pumps, and, of course, her pearls.

"Oh hey, Kate," I said, refraining from the question foremost in my mind: what the hell are you doing here? On a list of people least likely to show that night, Kate Brady would have been topped only by her aunt Dottie and uncle Chris Cole, owners of KBAY, which broadcast from offices in Garnet, ninety miles south on the bay. "Glad you could make it," I added. I was, after all, something of a hostess.

"Frankly, I can't believe I'm even here," she said, frowning. "I mean, a sock hop? I think I must be coming down with, what do they call that, cabin flu."

"Fever. Cabin fever."

Kate was fairly new in town herself, lured—most unwillingly by her account—to help out at KBAY. She was from someplace in New England, one of those places where everyone went to prep school and wore pearls and lived by rules I didn't even know existed. I did not necessarily understand the difference between her world and mine, only that the difference existed, and from her perspective, I inhabited the lower rung.

"So hey, way to go on the DUI," she said. "You should have heard my uncle when he saw it come over the wire with your name on it. Fuck, you would have thought it was Teddy Kennedy and Chappaquiddick all over again. Personally, I don't see what the big deal is. The guy's a has-been. It's so not news."

She said it all in a rush, and then she paused and looked at me, as if to say, your turn.

That's when I realized ours were the only voices in the otherwise quiet crowd. The twist had ended, and Denny was front and center on stage welcoming everyone. Di stood next to him, two-year-old little Billy on her hip. He introduced the two, then singled out a few of the bay's big shots, most notably Annie and Jack, our latest testament to the powers of radio.

"Oh my god, how lame is that?" Kate said, clearing her throat. I put a finger to my lips again. She muttered, slightly more quiet this time, "She lost a load of hay from her pickup? What is this, *Green Acres*?"

"Annie has horses," I whispered.

"So."

"So, she lost the load of hay and Jack stopped to help her, then drove off before she could thank him. Denny said something about it on the air. Jack heard it and called in. Now they're a pair. It's a nice story," I said.

"Hmph. Just lovely. But I'm sorry, I just can't believe this place. Forget that it's so small a town it's beyond laughable. The place is lost in the past. Like this sock hop. What the hell?"

"But here you are," I said.

"Oh, well thank you very much, Miss Manners. Lighten up, for cripe's sake. We're all stuck in this shithole together. Of course, you probably think it's perfectly normal to host a fifties dance a hundred years after the fact." And then she crossed her arms over her chest and frowned at me, as if to ask, now why did you have to make me do that?

"Pete? Where's Pete," Denny called from the stage. "Pete, you out there?"

"Oh my God, he wants you up on stage," Kate said, smacking my arm with the back of her hand. "Break a leg, pal."

Denny watched me cut through the crowd, straightening his leather jacket and smoothing the hair he wore in a pompadour like a young Elvis. Mitch, our wildly smart, somewhat nuts evening DJ, stopped bobbing on the balls of his feet long enough to stretch out a hand and pull me up on stage.

"Everyone, our news director, Pete Nash," Denny said.

"If you listen to Pete mornings," Denny continued, lapsing into an accent somewhere between Boston and the Bronx, "you might have noticed she's not from around here. You know what they say about truth being stranger than fiction? Try this one: Pete graduated from her Joisey high school at seventeen. By then, she'd been at Rocky's Sub Shop three years. Rocky hears you can't get a good

East Coast sub in Alaska and persuades Pete to come up and help him open a new shop. Six months later, Rocky's sick of the mosquitoes and rain. He hangs up the Closed sign once and for all and goes home. Pete stays.

"No kidding. And that's how Pete, who'd never been farther than the Jersey Shore, got to Alaska. And that's how I knew Pete was going to make one helluva newswoman. She's got the moxie."

I looked out over the hall and seeing everyone smiling—their reflections glittering in the mirror ball—for a second forgot about the blues shadowing my heart and remembered how lucky I was just to be here.

We climbed from the stage. Elvis came over the speakers, "Wise men say . . ."

Di passed Billy off to a woman I recognized as her babysitter, then reached for Denny's hand, giving her poodle skirt a little twirl and lifting a hand to the ash-blonde hair curling above her shoulder in a sixties flip.

Di was a little thing with a perfect figure, a heart-shaped face, and a chipped front tooth. More attractive than pretty, sweet unless crossed. Di helped with sales and occasionally did the voiceovers for ads, which she wasn't very good at, though only Jeremy dared say as much. She had jettisoned an entire life—twin sons, husband, successful small business—after catching Denny in his Elvis revue show seven years earlier. Denny had been a forty-year-old confirmed bachelor when she came into his life. He instantly christened her Di, latching onto the starry romance of Charles and Diana, and we never called her anything but. Denny adored his Di. And she adored him, too. For a time, anyway.

Denny took her hand and leaned in to kiss her just as Lydia Merit strode through the door, swishing her way toward us in a shirtwaist dress that would have made June Cleaver green.

"I better go make nice," Denny said, breaking into a big smile and opening his arms wide as if he could hug even from afar.

Lydia owned Merit Ford and the Wrassell Friendly Mall and was by far our biggest advertiser. She was thin as a stick figure with razor-sharp black hair. But what really defined Lydia was her fervent belief in the Lord Almighty, which led her to punctuate her sentences with phrases like "Praise God" and "Glory be." We tried very hard not to offend Lydia's tender sensibilities. But when we did, say with a mildly off-color joke on the air, it was a sure bet the phone would be ringing and Denny would have to soothe and cajole. But Lydia was also strangely flirtatious, and Denny knew just how to play her.

We watched Denny charm his way across the floor.

Di wiggled her fingers in Lydia's direction. I lifted my hand and faked an enthusiastic we're-so-glad-you're-here smile. Then I spotted Jeremy striding our way, long limbs loose with a lazy kind of sureness. He was not a good-looking guy, but he possessed a certain confidence that seemed to make up for it.

I nudged Di.

"Great," she said. "Just what I need."

"I thought Denny had a talk with him?"

"Oh, he had a talk with him, all right. Now, instead of criticizing me every time I open my mouth, he's going to be my coach."

"Seriously? How's that going to work?"

"Fine," she said with a smirk. "I'm going to meet with him in the production room a couple of times a week. And he's going to teach this little town hick how they do radio in the big city."

I looked at her and grinned, "This should be good."

"So Pete," Jeremy said, now standing before us, one hand stuck in the back pocket of his jeans, "I'm pretty sure they weren't wearing heels with their bobby socks back in the day."

"Sure they were," Di said, eyebrows raised, still that smirk. "The cool girls anyway."

"Oh really," Jeremy said. "So what does that make you?"

"That makes me the mother of three who is no longer interested in being cool," Di said.

"Is that so?" Jeremy said.

"It is," Di said.

"Well then," he said, extending a hand, "it's been a long time since I danced with a girl in saddle shoes. What do you say?"

Di's mouth opened and froze, her brown eyes widened. "Oh," she said. Then, regaining her cool, she smiled and let him take her hand.

I watched the dance floor for awhile—Denny charming Lydia as he spun and dipped her; Di and Jeremy, all smiles and good behavior; and next to them, Kyle, our afternoon jock, and Skye, the Wings 'N Things delivery girl, looking much too intent for a married man and a single woman.

Another thirty minutes and I figured I'd have done my share for the cause. I'd be free to go home, curl up in front of the woodstove, and write Nate, something I did almost daily, though there was precious little to report.

The Pepsi delivery guy caught me off guard with a request to dance, and I let him whirl me around for the last bit of a song before escaping to the ladies' room.

I tugged open the heavy door and found Annie standing before the mirror brushing the long auburn-colored hair that fell halfway down her back.

Annie was the owner of Wrassell Annie's Tavern, a widow who'd lost her husband to the sea as a newlywed. Everyone knew Annie, and generally everyone loved her. And me, well, I just wanted to be like her. Annie was an outdoorswoman, a tall, willowy woman who hunted her own game and packed it home on horseback. She shot skeet and raced snowmobiles. She was rich and pretty, goodhearted and perfectly content in her own skin. She was, I thought, the woman Nate hoped I'd grow to be.

I had taken my cues for dress from *Grease*, blue-jean capris, oversized white man's shirt found for a couple of bucks at the Salvation Army, white anklets, and black patent leather heels. Annie had more of a Dale Evans thing going with a knee-length skirt and gold nugget belt buckle. Not my style, but I might have readily converted for her boots—dark brown leather, pointy-toed things with flourishes of teal and white and a price tag I was guessing was well into the triple digits.

Annie caught my gaze.

"They're a little much, trust me, hon, I know. But I ain't had a serious suitor in a long time. I figured it called for something special, so I flew down to Seattle last weekend to do me a little shopping."

"So," I said, eyeing her in the mirror with something of a challenge. "It is serious, huh? Denny'll love that."

"Well, now don't you go getting all fired up. I have enough trouble with Denny as it is. I swear, the man would have us marry tomorrow if we gave him half the chance. And probably persuade us to do it live on the air, if I know him." She paused, gathering her hair in one hand, then clipped it in a sterling silver and turquoise barrette.

"But yeah, since you ask, Pete. I suppose it is. But you see, that's what scares me. I've gotten to where I'm pretty good on my own."

"Really? You don't get lonely? Don't miss having someone around?" I asked.

"Well, sure I did. But you adjust. And then one day you realize you've come to like your time alone, that you can be pretty good company in your own right. Know what I mean?"

I looked at her and sighed, "Not me."

"Trust me," she said. "Give it time. That husband of yours will be back in no time and then you'll find yourself missing the solitude."

The door flew open and banged against the wall.

"Whew. It's warm out there," Di said, fanning her face.

"Warm? You must be running a fever, hon," Annie said. "Either that, or you just had a hot dance with Elvis."

I laughed. "She was dancing with Jeremy."

"Good heavens, you two," Di said, frowning. "I'm just warm, all right?" She pulled a compact from her purse and powdered her nose.

Annie finished with her lipstick. "I just realized I haven't seen hide nor hair of those handsome young twins of yours. I thought they were coming in for the big dance this weekend?"

"Changed my mind. The holidays were so unbearable, I decided there's really no reason to spend all that money to fly them here if they're just going to make everyone miserable. They're awful to Denny, and he doesn't help matters."

"Poor things, probably just bored," Annie said. "We ought to take them hunting sometime when they visit."

"Hunting? Are you kidding, Annie, my boys have never even held a gun, and I wouldn't trust them if they did."

"Of course you would. You teach them safety and responsibility. And speaking of guns, you know, I've been thinking, we oughta plan ourselves a girls' hunting weekend next moose season." Di and I exchanged a glance.

"Oh come on," Annie said, frowning. "You gals would love it. We'll take the horses on up to my cabin, hunt during the day, drink a little wine, play some Scrabble at night. By the end of the weekend, if we're lucky, we'll have enough moose for all of our freezers."

"The only thing I've ever hunted was a good sale at Nordies," I said.

"Seriously," Di said.

"Ah, come on you two. This is Alaska. You gotta get outdoors, experience nature."

"What kind of gun would I need?" I asked. I'd never hunted a day in my life and I'd never planned to, either, but Annie was sort of local royalty and it felt like an honor just to be asked.

"Any large caliber rifle will do, Pete. Ask that handsome husband of yours. Me, I'd say a .300 mag or a .30-06 should do it."

"I think you're out of your mind, dearie," Di said. "Though I must say the idea of a weekend away from Billy and Denny and housework and every other thing for which I seem to be responsible sounds heavenly. Maybe I'll just come along and cook. The rest of you can get out and kill things."

"All right then, ladies," Annie said, "we have ourselves a deal. This fall, we're going hunting."

Out on the dance floor, Denny spotted me and waved impatiently. I hurried to meet him across the room where he stood with Lydia and a few other chamber of commerce types.

"I've been looking all over for you," Denny said. "Listen, Walter here says there's something going on out at the Cabaret. There's a bunch of cops, an ambulance. You better go check it out."

Check it out? We never chased ambulances and sure as hell not on a Saturday night. By the time I got there, I'd be damned near home. And odds were it was nothing more than an accident. Driver wipes out on black ice. Car collides with moose. Drunk wraps car around tree.

Walter, an insurance agent, gave me an apologetic look. And that's when I got it, Denny had an audience. There'd be no getting out of this one.

I grabbed my parka from the entry coat rack and walked across the parking lot, muttering all the things I would have liked to say to Denny. Then I remembered, Brady. Where the hell was Brady? I scanned the parking lot for the wood-paneled Cherokee with the KBAY lettering but didn't see it. Shit. Did she know? Was she already out there? I hurried to the Scout, climbed in, and turned the key. The engine whined. Shit. I had been wrong. It was too cold. I should have plugged her in. I turned the key again, foot stomping on the gas pedal, begging, but the engine grew ever weaker.

Denny spotted me coming back through the doors and frowned.

"I thought you were out of here?" Denny said.

"My battery's dead," I said.

"Ah, Pete, how can you cover the news when you can't even get to the scene?" He waited, as if I might actually have an answer to that.

"So, what are you going to do?" he said, finally. The others watched, looking mildly peeved, as if I had somehow failed them, too.

"I could take the Suburban," I tried.

"What? Are you kidding me? The Suburban?" He turned to his audience. "You hear that. The kid wants me to lend her a $20,000 custom rig. Do I look insane?"

"I'd be happy to give you a ride . . ." Until then, I hadn't even noticed him.

Ren met me out front in a faded red Mercedes I recognized from the used car lot, where it had sat for as long as I could remember. I climbed in and gave him directions.

Twenty minutes later I pointed to the lights swirling around the parking lot of the Cherry Cabaret.

"Seriously," Ren said, gripping the wheel in his black leather gloves and staring in a sort of no-kidding wonder. "A strip joint all the way out here?"

"It's Alaska," I said. "There's always a strip joint."

I passed the club every day on my way in and out of town. There were always at least a few cars in the parking lot. In the winter, it was the locals, the young guys, the divorced, the widowed, the married guys who never got any at home. Summer months, it was the tourists, the men at the campgrounds suddenly remembering the bag of ice, the cigarettes, the cream for their morning coffee they'd forgotten and slipping off to town.

A group of girls in high heels, cheap furs, and big hair stood huddled together, clutching cigarettes and shaking in the cold. A couple of them were local girls, but mostly the dancers were the girls the owner, Bud, brought in from his other clubs. Bidarkee Bay was sort of the Siberia of the strip joint circuit, the place you were exiled to when you got out of line—or the place you fled to when you needed to lay low.

I pushed open the Mercedes door and started in their direction. The girls eyed me, hackles up. Then I saw her, standing a bit off by herself. I looked again. A third time. Holy hell. Bobbie? It was her alright.

I'd met her in Anchorage in a place called the TC—formally, The Treasure Chest, commonly, the titty club. I was broke. Anchorage was full of bars, and you could make good money in tips. Better than you'd get from the cheap asses who ate in places like Denny's. And it was daily money. But I had no cocktail experience, and I couldn't get hired on even at the dumps. The TC was hiring. It was that or starve, that or go back home to the crummy little New Jersey town where I grew up, where a good life was a job at the factory and summer weekends at the shore.

The TC was downtown on a nasty street where no one with any sense walked at night. Guys from the local motorcycle club kept things in order; the slob of an owner kept an eye on the girls from the back office. No one paid me much mind.

I didn't dance and I didn't undress. And I can tell you no one wants to tip the only clothed girl in a strip joint. Some of the dancers took pity on me—the nineteen-year-old, naïve-as-hell kid—and dropped a little cash in my jar when they were having a good night. Bobbie wasn't one of them. She pretty much ignored me. Then one evening I went in to the TC straight from my day job of selling and teaching ballroom dancing—a commission-only gig, which should tell you something about my paycheck. I went into the back room to change out of my Danskin skirt and body suit into my jeans and V-neck and found Bobbie, pacing, smoking, looking pissed. She was a tall girl, long straight brown hair, and eyes that were neither green nor blue, but both. She was beautiful, about three years older than I, I guessed, but decades older in worldliness.

"What are you doing in a hole like this, anyway?" she'd asked.

"I could ask you the same," I said. I had learned young that the only way to handle someone throwing their weight around was to throw some around yourself.

"Don't be stupid," Bobbie said. "I'm making money. I'm going to grad school."

"I do OK," I said, which was laughable. "And I'm planning to go to school myself." It was something I had just begun to think about it.

"Sure," she said. "By the way, nice outfit," gesturing to my burgundy Danskins. I had two sets, one burgundy, one black. Mixing and matching, I could get four outfits out of them.

"Thanks," I said, thinking maybe she was warming up to me just a little.

"Those are what the real dancers wear, huh," she said, smirking.

I just shrugged and went out front to serve drinks.

The next night I showed up for work and immediately went to the back room for the Danskins I'd left behind the night before. They were gone. So was Bobbie. I lasted another two weeks at the place. Then I found a better job, gave up the ballroom lark, and started school.

And now, all this time, all this way, here she was. And I was still pissed about my Danskins. "Hey," I said, drawing close.

She nodded, eyeing the mic and recorder. "Something I can do for you?"

"I was hoping you could tell me what's going on."

She looked at me, harder now. Then, "Do I know you?" she asked.

"Not really," I said. "A few years back I worked at the TC. It's Bobbie, isn't it?"

She had just inhaled and now she choked on the smoke, coughing hard into her hand, eyes watering.

But Bobbie was good. "Damned menthols," she said, tapping a hand against her chest. "They're too strong for me. I'm sorry, you were saying."

"I waitressed at the TC."

"Huh? The TC? Heard of it, but sorry—"

"You, umm, borrowed my Danskins," I said.

A corner of her mouth twitched, and I thought for a second she might laugh out loud. But she just shook her head, "You've got the wrong chick, honey. My name's Robyn." Robyn? Was she serious. Just that easy she could pretend to be someone else?

"Hmmm, my mistake," I said, playing along. No sense in pissing her off. If anyone knew anything about what was going on, it was probably Bobbie.

She took another hit off the slender white cigarette, then tapped it with a long red nail and watched the ash fall. She exhaled. "No problem. Guess I must have a twin somewhere out there. We all do you know."

"Well hey, I work for the radio station, KWLD. Wondering if you know anything about what's going on."

She lifted her cigarette in the direction of three rows of single wides. Next to the trailers was a patch of scraggly evergreens and tangled brush. An officer was wrapping yellow tape around the perimeter of trees. Flashlight beams glared and crossed each other and a spotlight lit up an area just beyond the edge of the brush. "Someone said they found something. A body, maybe."

She glanced down at my mic. "But you didn't hear that from me."

"Do you know . . ." I started.

"Wait, I don't want to be in the news."

"That's cool," I said. "It's not running."

"But I don't want even my name on a piece of paper," she said.

"OK, fine, but do they know who it is or anything?"

She shrugged, clutched her collar tighter, and took a deep breath. "You didn't hear this from me, OK? I don't want anything to do with anything."

"Got it."

"One of our girls has been missing. Jillian Berry. No one's seen her for at least a week. We all figured she probably just skipped out on her contract."

She looked away for an instant. "I'm afraid it might be her." She ran her index finger gently under one eye, then the other.

"I don't know if you heard, but there's a serial killer out there," she said. "The cops won't admit it, but everyone knows."

The rumors had been circulating around Anchorage for some time. More than just rumors, there were bodies found in shallow graves. Dancers gone missing. But no one was saying if they were connected or if the girls were truly missing or had just disappeared willingly to get away from the creeps who ran the clubs. Like Bobbie, I guessed.

"So you think it's true?" I asked. "You think there's some crazy killer out there murdering strippers?"

"Dancers," she corrected. "Oh heck yeah I believe it. There's definitely some nut out there. Maybe more than one. You know the whack jobs that come in these places."

I raised an eyebrow.

"I mean everyone does," she said.

"But here on the bay? Why would he come here?"

"Why not? Ted Bundy murdered women in seven different states. Did you know that?"

"No actually, I guess I didn't."

"Oh sure, guys like him operate all over the place. The police don't care because we're not," she made quotation marks with her fingers, "nice girls."

We heard a voice call out from the woods, then watched as two men emerged, wheeling a stretcher between them. On top was a long black plastic bag. The body. I felt the skin on my arms prickle and rise.

A car pulled into the lot behind us. Bobbie shielded her eyes against the light. A guy stepped from the car. It was a big car, older, but one of those that had probably been a prize a decade before.

"That's my ride," she said. She started toward him, then turned. "What's your name again?"

"Pete. Pete Nash."

"Nice meeting ya, Pete." And then she gave a little laugh. "Danskins, huh? I had a pair of those. Burgundy. Come to think of it,

I don't know what happened to them. Someone must have stolen them." She wiggled her red fingertips in what was to pass for a wave and hurried away.

I watched for an instant. I had dodged a bullet. I had been young and stupid enough to walk through the doors of a place like the TC and somehow get the hell out. I had worked with Bobbie and had lost nothing more than a skirt and top.

I started toward the woods. The ambulance moved through the parking lot, lights swirling, sirens quiet. No hurry.

Chief Romer stood alone, watching the scene around him.

"Chief Romer," I called.

He looked toward me. I waved.

The chief and I had gotten to know each other the summer before during a labor strike. He was there to make sure the two sides didn't kill each other, and I was there to report it if they did. I told him about growing up back East and he told me about growing up Tlingit, and we both commiserated on our desire to smoke.

He ducked under the yellow tape and walked to meet me.

"Ah hell, Pete, I was hoping I'd at least have 'til morning before I had to deal with you reporters," he said, pulling out the coffee stir stick he chewed on in place of a cigarette.

"Sorry," I said.

He swiped a hank of black hair from his eyes, planted his hands on his hips, and studied the ground. Then, "And what are you wearing on your feet?"

I looked down at my high heels, the bare calves between my capris and white anklets. "I didn't have time to change," I said.

He clicked his tongue, "You'll break your neck."

"OK if I run a tape?" I asked, fingers already poised on the Play/Record buttons on the tape player hanging by my side.

"If you must, but there's not going to be much I can tell you."

I held the mic toward him. "Can you tell us what happened out here tonight, Chief," I asked, channeling the TV reporters Denny nagged me to watch.

"Well, we got a call tonight from one of the tenants here at the trailer park. He said he'd been noticing a bad smell that was getting worse. Then tonight his dog returned with a woman's high heel. He was afraid to take a look himself. We sent an officer to check things out."

He paused. I waited.

"About ten yards back, he found a shallow grave. Body of a woman. Animals had gotten into it."

"Jeez," I said. "That's awful."

"Yup. Lucky we found it when we did."

"Do you know who it was? Someone said a girl from the club is missing."

"I'm not going to speculate on that."

"Do you know how she died?"

"Sorry, Pete. We'll have to wait for the autopsy."

"Do you think it has anything to do with what's been going on in Anchorage? The missing dancers . . ."

The chief held up a hand. "Whoa, it's way too soon to be going down that road. I think that's about as much as I'm going to say tonight."

I knew better than to push, that I was lucky to have gotten what I did. I clicked off the recorder.

"Thanks, Chief," I said, starting for the Mercedes. Then I remembered and turned to him again. "Hey Chief, any other reporters been by?"

"Just your friend from KBAY."

Shit. I knew it.

"Just kidding," he called. "But hey, get yourself some decent winter boots, huh?"

Back at the station, I dialed the AN and told the night editor what I had.

"Huh?" he said. "Sounds like the others they found in the valley."

"That's what I was thinking. And there's a stripper from the Cabaret no one's seen for awhile. The club's right out in front of the lot where she was found."

"Hmmm. The girls here were found outside of town. Then again, you're on the bay. I guess everything there is pretty much outside of town. Go ahead, give me what you've got."

I read the story I'd scribbled on the drive back, then hung up and typed up a couple other versions of the story so the jocks wouldn't have to read the same one every time. I didn't have much audio to use, but I had enough. I looked around the newsroom for a couple of blank cartridges. They looked like the old eight-tracks but held only enough tape for thirty seconds to a couple of minutes. You transferred bits and pieces of the sound from the cassette player or reel-to-reel onto the carts to play with the story you were reading. But that night I was out of blanks. I walked down the hall to the production room, reached inside the door, and flipped the light switch. Someone yelled and I jumped and let out a little yell, too, then found myself facing Kyle and Skye, nestled in the bean bag chair, fumbling with their clothes.

"Shit, you scared the crap out of me," I said.

"You?" Kyle said, hand to heart. "You about gave me a heart attack." Next to him Skye fastened a button on her blouse and smoothed her hair.

"Don't mind me, I just wanted to get some blank carts," I said.

"Uh sure, help yourself," Kyle said, looking sheepish now. He was a thirty-ish-year-old guy, balding, shaped like an eggplant. He had a wife and kid in the Lower 48 who were supposed to join him as soon as he saved the money for airline tickets.

Skye looked up at me and smiled, "Sorry, we didn't mean to startle you." She was a plump woman who believed in the power of crystals, psychics, and anything connected to Shirley MacLaine.

She wasn't the kind you expected to be screwing someone else's husband.

I grabbed a couple of carts.

"See you," I said, flipping the room back to darkness.

"Pete," Kyle called.

"Yeah?"

"You won't say anything."

"What's there to say?"

"Thanks," he said.

I walked back to the newsroom. Ren had disappeared. I would have to figure out another ride. First, I wanted to see my story. But the wire sat quiet. I sighed. Maybe they had decided not to run it after all. What passed for big news out here was often just the everyday grind in Los Anchorage.

"Knock, knock," Ren said from the doorway.

"You're still here?" I said.

"Of course. You thought I left? I'm sorry. I thought you heard me say I'd be right back." He held my moon boots toward me. "If your feet didn't freeze already."

"My boots. Thank you. I was wondering how I was going to get to those."

"Come on, I'll give you a ride home."

We were halfway down the stairs when Cork, the night jock, caught up with us and handed me the latest offering from the wire.

"Breaking News, Contributed by Pete Nash, KWLD, Wrassell, Bidarkee Bay "Woman's Body Found in Shallow Grave."

Ren opened the car door for me, waited for me to get situated, then closed it. He was that kind of guy. Nate was a polite guy, opened doors, that kind of thing, but there was a formality with Ren, a sense that he'd learned such mannered behavior right along with his first steps.

"Thanks for the ride," I said. "You really saved my butt."

"Happy to. Certainly much more exciting than hanging out watching the limbo."

I laughed and he laughed with me.

"I've been meaning to ask. Is Pete short for something?"

"Patrice," I said.

"It's a lovely name."

"It's not me," I said. "No one calls me that."

"Then perhaps I could be the first."

I gave him a look.

"Then again, maybe not," he said, fixing me with a boyish smile.

We drove in silence for a while. I was tired and suddenly aware again that this guy was a complete stranger. He, I sensed, felt awkward alone with me in the close space of the car, no crime to race to, just us and the night.

For a second time that night, we came upon the Cherry Cabaret, its pink-and-red neon flashing against the night. A couple of police cars sat at the edge of the parking lot, and a couple lights still glowed from the woods.

"You know, we never have murders here," I said.

"Never?"

"Well, rarely and then it's usually one of those somebody-done-somebody-wrong kind of things. Husband catches wife with best friend. Or cabin fever and booze."

"Cabin fever?"

"People get all kinds of crazy in the winter here. That's why you gotta stay busy, get out. Otherwise, the dark and cold will drive you nuts."

"I see. I'll keep it in mind."

"Running an inn will probably keep you busy enough," I said. "When do you plan to open?"

He looked at me, kind of with that same busted look Kyle had shot me earlier.

"I'm not . . . it's not . . ."

"Oh. You're not? So why did you tell Denny?"

He shook his head. "I didn't. Not really. That was just some-thing Denny and I talked about over beers one night. You know, the potential, how if someone wanted to . . . Bar talk. I had no idea he was going to tell the world."

"Yeah, Denny's like that. So, why are you here?"

"I have to have a reason?"

"No, but not a lot of people choose winter to visit."

"No kidding. I guess I wasn't thinking about the timing. I just wanted to see the place. My grandfather built it. My mother used to talk about it all the time. But my father wanted no part of it. My father, for the record, was a world-class bastard."

I looked at him, surprised. It wasn't something I expected from him. But then, I'd learn Ren was full of surprises.

"How long are you staying?" I asked.

"Oh, not long I shouldn't think."

"You ought to stay at least 'til after breakup. See the midnight sun, go fishing."

"Breakup?"

"It's what they call spring everywhere else. Everything melts and turns muddy and wet. Pretty big mess for awhile."

"Lovely. Sorry I won't be able to stick around for it," he said, chuckling.

"It passes," I said.

"Hey, you're a ways out here, aren't you."

"We're almost there," I said. "Sorry."

"No, not at all. I'm going to guess you don't live all the way out here alone?"

I told him about Nate's new job.

"Not until May," he said. "Wow. I would think Wrassell would be a pretty bleak place to winter alone."

"It probably will be," I said. "But I'll survive."

"I'm sure you will," he said, fixing me with that grin again.

"You'll want to start looking for a little road just up here on the right." And then, "Here, right here."

He tapped the brakes and took a sharp turn onto the dirt road, and I directed him to the lake.

"I'm sorry, is there supposed be a road or something?" he asked.

"It's a shortcut," I told him.

"A shortcut? You mean over the lake?"

"It's frozen."

"I see that."

He eased the car onto the ice, then stopped. "You do this often?"

"All the time."

And it was true, I must have crossed over that lake two, three, even four times some days. I crossed it so much I didn't even think anymore about the fact that it was a lake.

"If you just point it straight for the other end, eventually you'll wind up right where you need to be," I said.

"If you say so," he said and gave the Mercedes gas. He started to relax. And then we heard it. A bump. Then a bigger bump. Then a drop, like falling in a pothole, the sound of ice crunching beneath the tires. I realized what was happening right about the same time he did.

"Fuck," I said. "The ice is breaking."

Ren braked. The Mercedes shuddered to a stop.

Panic started somewhere in the core of my being and spread through me like electricity. We couldn't go back to the shore, the ice behind us was already broken. To the left, the bank was steep and rocky, impossible to drive over. To the right, the shore was too distant to see.

"Drive, Ren. Just drive," I yelled.

"But Pete . . ."

"We've got to get off the ice."

He started forward. The night grew quiet again, the ice once more seemed solid. I started to calm, to feel embarrassed even. What a pair of chickens we were. And then came a new crack, a crack like the whole world was splitting open. No mere patch of bumpy ice this, but the entire continent that was the lake. We were going to fall through. In that water, we would last maybe five minutes before the cold shut down our hearts. And who would find us? Ever? There was nothing to do but keep going. Ren stared grimly ahead, hands tight on the wheel. My heart pounded. And then, long minutes later, I saw the spot of yellow from the streetlight on our road.

"There, the road's right there," I said, my voice quivering.

It wasn't until we pulled into the driveway that I think either of us dared to breathe. He turned off the car, then leaned back against the seat and exhaled long and deep.

"I am so sorry," I said. "Nate said it was safe. It's always been safe."

He reached over and took my hand. And there we sat, hand in hand, two strangers processing the idea that we had just very nearly died.

"You know," he said, "I can think of a lot of ways to die. But freezing to death in an ice-covered lake and then drowning would not be my first choice. Somehow, it seems doubly cruel."

"I am so sorry," I said again. "I don't understand . . . Nate would have never said, if it wasn't safe."

He gave my hand a squeeze. "Do you always attract this much drama?" I turned to him and saw that he was smiling. And we both laughed. Finally.

"Hey, I better get inside and get the fire going before the pipes freeze. Or else there really will be some drama."

I climbed out. He met me at the front of the car and walked me to the porch.

I pushed open the door.

"You don't lock your door?" he said, following me inside.

"The locks don't work right. Nate says the house is still settling. And like I said, we don't really have a lot of crime on the bay. Out here, the biggest thing that ever happens is the local kids stealing cars for joyriding and dumping them in the woods."

"Still, after tonight, you might want to reconsider that," he said.

"I guess that's true. Except I'm not a stripper or prostitute, so if it is a serial killer, I don't imagine he'll be too interested in me."

"Brrrr," he said. "You're right. It's absolutely freezing in here."

"It'll just take a minute. It warms up fast," I said.

"You don't have heat?"

"Of course we have heat," I said, pointing to the woodstove.

"Oh," he said, "of course."

I could tell he thought it was nuts. I walked to the woodstove, put in the hearth log, the newspaper, cardboard, my teepee of kindling, then struck the match. Once it caught, I set in the bigger pieces, careful not to smoother the growing flames.

"You chop your own wood and everything?"

"Just the kindling. Nate left me a supply of wood that should last through the winter."

He grinned. "Just the kindling, huh."

"I should probably make more effort to chop the bigger stuff, but I'm pretty lousy with an ax."

"Thanks for the warning," he said. Then, "Cute little place."

"Nate built it."

I loved our little cabin. It was nothing, but it was ours. It was a beginning. It was home. But now looking around, I wondered what Ren saw. Just about everything was either handmade or second hand. Nate got the hardwood floors from the old high school gym. We'd rescued the tile from the dump where Nate had watched a man unload boxes of the stuff, most of it perfectly good. Never did figure out why someone would do something like that. The furniture, an old rocker and a sofa, came from garage sales. We had one closet. Not even a bedroom, just the loft upstairs with a box spring and mattress, as much as would fit.

I closed the door on the woodstove.

"Can I offer you something to drink?" I said. It seemed the polite thing to do after he'd driven me around all night and then I'd damned near gotten us killed on the lake. Though what I really wanted to do was finish the letter to Nate I seemed always to be working on.

"Yes, that would be nice."

"I've got some white zin," I said.

He bit his lower lip. "Uh, sure."

"Wait. Maybe . . ." I walked to the kitchen and looked beneath the counter where we kept the pots and pans, dishes, food. I pulled from the corner a half full bottle of Crown Royal. "I have this," I said, holding it up.

"Perfect."

I tapped myself a glass of white zin from the box in the fridge and poured him a healthy measure of Crown over ice in a juice glass. I gave him the glass and took the opposite end of the sofa.

He spotted my stack of books.

"Fitzgerald fan?"

"I love Fitzgerald," I said.

"Me too. There's always so much yearning in F. Scott."

Yearning. I hadn't known. I would have to think about that.

He took a sip of his drink, then leaned back in the sofa. I heard him murmur something. At first I thought he was talking to himself, but then his voice grew more certain and clear.

"*Let us go then, you and I, / When the evening is spread out against the sky . . . / Of restless nights in one-night cheap hotels / And sawdust restaurants with oyster-shells.*"

It was a poem. The men I knew didn't recite poetry, didn't even know poetry unless you counted Robert Service, and I didn't know exactly what I was supposed to do.

He stopped and turned to me. "'The Love Song of J. Alfred Prufrock.' Do you know it?"

"I don't think so," I said. Which was a lie. I had no idea.

"T. S. Eliot," he said.

I nodded. I fancied myself a pretty serious reader, but that night I began to understand how little I knew.

I let out a yawn, unexpected and loud. I covered my mouth in embarrassment. "I am so sorry. I don't know where that came from."

"I guess I better let you get some sleep," he said, glancing toward me with a raised eyebrow. I could tell he was hoping I would say no.

"Now that you mention it, I am beat."

He sat forward, "Uh, just one problem."

"What?" I asked.

"How do I get out of here," he chuckled. "Because surely you're not going to tell me I have to drive back over that lake."

I laughed too. "There's a road, you just follow it around the lake out to the highway. But go slow. The potholes are killers."

I slept a heavy, dreamless sleep and awoke in the morning with the realization that I was stranded. It was a good two miles to the nearest house, and I wasn't even sure anyone lived there in the winter. If not, I would just have to keep going until I found someone at home, or got out to the highway. It could take hours, and given the clear sky, I was pretty certain the temperatures had fallen to their normal frigid January lows. Then I spotted the snowmobile.

I slipped into my bibs and boots, grabbed my coat and gloves and the various other layers I'd need, and went outside. The snowmobile sat by the woodpile and was protected by a fitted black cover with Arctic Cat in white script. I pulled off the cover and knelt one knee on the black vinyl seat, turned the key, and pulled the cord. Nothing. It was always a bitch to start, and I wasn't entirely sure I could do it, which may have been just as well. The Cat was big and heavy, and if I did something stupid—like rolled it or got it stuck—I was on my own. I tried again anyway. And then I kept trying until I heard the beginnings of a purr and was finally rewarded with the steady hum of the engine. I pulled on the rest of my winter gear, climbed on, and took off down the road. The cold air nipped at the skin between my goggles and scarf. I was halfway to the highway when I saw the faded red of the Mercedes round a bend coming toward me.

I goosed the throttle and rode up to meet him.

Ren looked at me and then did one of those double takes: It's you. "Pete," he said with that amused smile of his. "Good morning."

"I am so happy to see you," I said.

"Really. Well good, I'm happy to see you, too."

"I mean, because, you know, I need a ride."

"You mean you're not happy to see me?"

"Yes, that, too. You know what I mean."

"I think so," he said, blue eyes crinkling with his smile.

THREE

On Monday, Chief Romer put out a press release identifying the body as that of Jillian Berry, the missing dancer. She had been shot once in the head. Later that day the AN ran a story speculating about the other missing dancers, the dead girls already found in shallow graves and the question of the serial killer.

On my way home that afternoon, I stopped at the Laundromat. Usually I did my wash over the weekend when the attendant was an old woman in a housedress and knee-high nylons who called all the other women Sis. But with everything going on that weekend I'd put it off. This evening the attendant working in the back was a tall, thin girl with a short dark pixie cut and hazel eyes. I had seen her before around town bartending but never before at the Laundromat. I didn't pay her any mind. I threw in my load of darks and a load of colors and hitched myself up on the folding table with *Gatsby* and a bottle of soda from the machine. The door creaked open and I heard her call his name.

"Ren, you're back," she said.

I glanced up as he closed the door behind him. She hurried from behind the counter to meet him, linking an arm through his.

"You haven't been in for a while, I was afraid . . ."

Ren glanced up and, seeing me, looked a little embarrassed. He let his arm fall from hers.

"Patrice," he said, grinning.

"Hey," I said.

"What's the big story today?"

"They ID'd the body. It was the dancer."

"Really."

I nodded.

"So what do you think, serial killer?"

"I don't know. I sure as hell hope not," I said, then added, "I'll never get any rest."

He chuckled.

"By the way, I talked to Nate about the lake. The ice is fine," I said. "It was just the top we broke through. He said it happens all the time. The surface melts under the sun, then starts to refreeze at night. There was still four, five feet of solid ice beneath that. At least."

I was pleased to be able to deliver this news, to validate my husband's claim of safety. But Ren just listened, shaking his head. "Seriously? You drove over it again?"

"Of course. It's fine."

"Jeez, Pete, I don't know whether to think you're really brave or just really stupid," he said.

And we both laughed.

I realized then that she was watching us, trying, it seemed, to figure out just who the hell I was.

She cleared her throat.

"Say, you two know each other?" Ren asked. And then, not waiting for our answer, "Pete, this is Belinda. Belinda, Pete."

"Hey," I said.

She gave me one of those wry half smiles and nodded, then took Ren's hand and led him to the back of the room. They reached the counter, and Belinda returned to her place behind it. Ren began pulling his white shirts from the valise he carried until there was a pile on the counter and then reached for his wallet and pulled out a slip of paper.

She took it and disappeared. Ren turned toward me.

"So how's *Gatsby*?" he asked.

"Yearning," I said.

He grinned. "Of course."

Belinda was back. He turned to her again, taking from her a package wrapped in brown paper. Moments later, they passed my way, her arm again linked through his, her voice teasing in a conversation I couldn't hear.

"See you, Pete," Ren called.

"Bye."

At the door, she let him go and walked backward, watching until he was gone. When she passed me, she glanced over, wearing a satisfied grin. And I realized that she thought I had a thing for Ren. I had to laugh, what a ridiculous idea.

A couple weeks went by and not another word about Jillian Berry. Not even rumors. If the cops knew anything, they were keeping it awfully quiet. Denny was obsessed with the story. It was ours and he was determined to keep it that way, which meant I lived in constant worry that something would break and Kate Brady would beat me to it.

That day, the day that would find me once again at the Cabaret, I finished the noon news and was getting ready to head out front to do the log books. By morning, I was the news director; by afternoon, I was the receptionist and traffic girl, which meant that between answering phone calls, I scheduled all the on-air promos and public service announcements, logging each one into the notebook by the hour it was to be played.

I heard a commotion outside the newsroom. There was Di overwhelmed in an ankle-length down coat, struggling with two large bags from Wings 'N Things and little Billy, wrapped for dear life around her neck.

I ran out and grabbed the bags from her.

"Thanks, hon," and then, "Jeez, Den, just stand there and watch why don't you?" Di called to Denny, who was in the lunchroom with Jeremy.

"Pete had it under control," he said. "You're fine."

As we drew closer he began to sing, "Oh where have you been Billy Boy . . ." Denny had a song for everyone. Di was his "Brown-eyed girl," With me, it was "East Coast girls are hip . . ." Billy lifted his head, a mass of blond ringlets, from Di's shoulder and whined. "Sssshh," Di hushed. "Billy doesn't want you to sing."

"Come here, Billy," Jeremy said, holding out his arms. "Let your buddy Jeremy hold you."

"Forget it," Denny said. "He's his daddy's boy."

Billy arched back from his mother's shoulder, and reached for Denny.

Denny hooked an arm under his bottom, tipped his head to the side to make room for Billy's cheek against his neck. "What did I tell you, Jer? Daddy's boy all the way."

I unloaded the bags and set the cartons of livers, gizzards, and hearts around the table. Wings 'N Things was one of our regular advertisers, and we all had a weakness for the deep fried, fat-laden poultry parts, which Di generally picked up on trade.

"So Pete, you talked to the cops today?" Denny asked.

I nodded.

"Anything?"

"On the stripper?"

"Well yeah, on the stripper. What else?"

"They're not saying anything," I said. "And yes, I ask."

"Hmph. That should tell you something in itself."

I tried to think what it was supposed to be telling me.

"If the cops aren't talking, you gotta go somewhere else. Right?"

"Umm right, I guess," I said.

"Like the strip joint? You try talking to anyone there?"

"Not yet," I said, as if it'd been something I'd been planning all along.

"Well, what are you waiting for?"

"Sure," I said. "I'll make some calls."

He frowned. "Oh for Pete's sake, Pete. You don't call a strip joint. You gotta go out there, talk to the man on the street. Or in this case, girls."

An hour later, I was turning into the Cherry Cabaret. I parked the Scout and took a look around the parking lot. It was mostly empty, as I hoped it would be at that hour. I hurried across the gravel, wanting only to get it over with, to go inside, find no one willing to talk, and get out of there. I didn't dare take the recorder and even my notebook I kept hidden in my coat pocket. And yes, it occurred to me, some reporter I was.

I pulled open the door. It was dark beyond dark, despite the glare of lights on the stage. There was a girl in a purple and red corset and matching thong doing a half-hearted swivel and grind to "Hungry Like the Wolf."

"Shut the fucking door," someone said.

I hadn't even realized it was open. I let it fall shut, but I stood where I was, hands jammed in my pockets, not sure what to do next.

"You here about the job, Cherie?" She was an older woman, with over-processed and over-teased hair, a powdered face, red lipstick, and false eyelashes that would have been laughable if she wasn't so scary. Bud's wife. I'd seen her around town driving the Caddie.

"Job? Me? No," I answered in a voice that did not sound like my own.

"I was just wondering . . ." I said, then started again, "I'm with KWLD . . ."

"It's OK, Cookie," someone called from behind me. I turned and saw Bobbie. "She's OK."

"Hey," I said.

She motioned for me to follow her. She was wearing a robe and flip-flops. Her hair was wet, her face bare. She stopped and leaned against a corner wall just out of sight from the rest of the room. "I don't have a lot of time. My shift starts soon. What do you need?"

"I just wanted to say I'm sorry about your friend," I said. "Have you heard anything more from the cops?"

"Well first, she wasn't really a friend," she said. "I mean, I barely knew her. She'd just got here a couple of weeks ago from Hawaii. And second, I told you, the cops don't care."

"I don't think that's true," I said. "Really."

"Honey, you don't have a clue. But here's the thing. No one is going to appreciate some news person out here digging up crap from their past. Know what I mean?"

It was the word *crap* that reminded me. Bobbie didn't swear. I remembered her telling one of other dancers at the TC that it made her sound cheap, and making a mental note that I could take a tip. Still, the irony. You don't expect lessons in manners from a stripper.

"I'm not trying to dig up anything," I said. "I'm just trying to do my job. I mean, wouldn't you like to know who killed her."

"Like, it's going to bring her back or something?" she asked, disdain just barely disguised.

"What if it was this serial killer?" I asked.

She seemed to consider something, then lightened a bit.

"I'll tell you what. If I hear anything, I'll tell you. But it works both ways. You hear anything, you come to me. Deal?"

"Sure," I lied. Like I'd just pop in every afternoon to exchange gossip with a bunch of females in G-strings?

But Bobbie believed in herself, in her charm, in her ability to get her way. I don't think it ever occurred to her that I wouldn't hold up my end of the deal. Then again, what was I thinking? Like Bobbie would?

Back on Melody Lane, I checked the newsroom like I always did. Just in case. But if there was any big news, we'd be the last to know. Wire copy spilled out of the cabinet, looping over itself in a jumble on the floor. Mitch and Kyle were both in the studio, one shift ending, the other about to begin. I shot them a dirty look. Someone was supposed to clear the wire when I was gone, and they knew it, but they were caught up in some deep discussion—no doubt over rock 'n' roll trivia, given the book Mitch waved around—and ignored me. I was tempted to trash the whole mess, but I was too afraid I'd miss something important, like Brady breaking a story. Deep in the middle of the jumble, somewhere between the Championship Sled Dog lineup and the latest marine weather forecast, I saw the headline: AN January Awards: Best Breaking Story—Pete Nash, KWLD, "Woman's Body Found . . ."

A couple of hours later, I pushed through the front door just as Ren climbed from the Mercedes. He saw me and broke into a big smile.

"You're here," he said. "I was afraid I'd missed you. Congratulations."

"You heard."

"Are you kidding? Everyone's heard. You didn't think Denny'd keep something like that quiet? Come on, I'll buy you a drink."

"Oh, I can't . . ." I said, formulating the excuse as I spoke.

"Come on, one drink," he said.

"Well . . . what the hell, why not," I said, suddenly brightened by the thought that there was something else besides home and my own company. "Annie's?"

"I have a better idea."

Fifteen minutes later, we pulled into the airport parking lot. I turned to him, puzzled. "The bar's really pricey here."

"It's my treat. And who said anything about the bar?"

"Then?"

"Trust me."

He cupped my elbow in his hand and walked me inside and down a corridor I hadn't known existed. We stopped outside a pair of frosted doors with gold lettering that read "The Gold Nugget Club" and below that "Members Only."

"It's a club for travelers," he said. "Where should we say we are going? Hawaii?"

"Everyone in Alaska goes to Hawaii," I said.

"Silly me, Hawaii, how clichéd. How about Paris by way of Seattle."

He pulled open the frosted door and held it for me, then guided me to a reception desk of glass and wood so polished it might have been metal.

"Mr. Kennedy, welcome. So good to see you," the receptionist said.

"Thank you," he said. "I have a guest today, Patrice Nash."

She jotted something in a book and handed his card back to him. "Enjoy your visit, Ms. Nash, Mr. Kennedy."

I waited until we cleared a second pair of doors, and turned to him, "It's Pete, Ren. No one calls me Patrice."

"But they should. They should."

Inside, everything was hushed and even though we could see the planes, the sound was muted. The carpet underfoot was extra thick, the music soft. People talked in lowered voices, ice cubes clinked. I didn't need to get on a plane to feel like I'd walked into a foreign place. Several people glanced up at us and then away. We were no one of importance.

I spotted the ladies' room and excused myself. Inside, I squared off before the mirror. Beige V-neck sweater. Jeans. Why hadn't I worn something nicer? I finger combed my curls and tugged them into shape, then tucked them back behind my ears. I touched up my foundation, penciled on a new line over my eyelids, brushed on some blush and freshened my lipstick. I checked my reflection again. I didn't exactly look like the sophisticated traveler, but it would have to do.

Ren had taken a small table and two chairs in a corner by the gas fireplace, opposite a wall of windows. He watched me approach, smiling. I think it was the first time I realized he had a thing for me, but I ignored that thought. It was of no matter. I was married.

"Come on, I'll get us a drink," he said. I followed him to a table covered in white linen and lined with bottles, Scotch, bourbon, gin.

"I'm sorry, I don't believe they have any of your pink zin," he said, then turned to me with a grin.

"You really don't like that wine, do you?"

"Oh, is that what it is?" he said, chuckling.

"Smart ass," I said.

"No, really. You should drink whatever you like. You realize I'm not serious?"

"Of course you are."

"OK, of course I am. How about a chardonnay?"

"Sure," I said.

He poured my wine and a Scotch for himself and filled a plate with crackers and cheese, and we walked back to the table he'd claimed.

Outside, a Lear jet taxied down the runway. Bidarkee Bay was a funny place that way, a lot of people just struggling to get by, but a lot of money, too. Texans with oil ties, mining execs, seafood traders, all slipping on and off the bay.

Ren pulled a pack of Salems from the inside pocket of his jacket.

"I didn't know you smoked," I said.

"I just took it up again, one of those pleasures I've decided I can afford. Would you like one?"

"I'd love one, but I can't."

"You sure?"

I nodded.

The jet lifted from the runway.

"My husband's a pilot, did I tell you that?"

"Really? No, I don't believe you did. Which airline?" He swirled the ice in his glass and sipped.

"He's a bush pilot."

"Yes, of course. Seems everyone here is," he said.

"Not everyone."

"Cheers," he raised his glass. "Here's to the best breaking news story."

I met his glass midway.

"You know, I wouldn't have gotten that story it if it hadn't been for you."

"Oh, you would have found a way. You have the . . . what was that Denny said? Oh yes, the moxie."

Then we both laughed, and it was in that moment I realized I genuinely liked the guy. I hardly knew him at all, and yet, already he felt like an old friend.

"So hey, how did you wind up at the radio station anyway?" he asked, after we'd stopped laughing.

"I applied for the receptionist position. Denny liked my voice, asked me if I wanted to give it a try."

"And you said yes, just like that?"

"Why not?"

"Why not, indeed. What's next? Think you'll stay in news?"

"TV, I think," I said.

"Really? I had you pegged for print."

"Why?"

He shrugged. "You're a Fitzgerald fan, for one. And every time I come by the station, you're hunched over the typewriter."

"But the real money's in television."

"But the real journalists are in print," he said. "Besides, money isn't everything."

"Oh yeah?" I said. "Try telling that to someone who doesn't have any." I told him about Denny's plans to start up a TV station on the bay. "He says I'll need to lose a few pounds, since the camera alone adds ten."

"Pete," he said, suddenly serious. "You don't need to lose weight. You have a beautiful figure."

"Oh no, Denny's right, I've always been . . ."

"Pete?" he said, grinning.

"Hmmm?"

"Just say thank you."

"Thank you," I said, embarrassed now.

"So, tell me about Pete."

"What do you want to know?"

He shrugged. "Everything. I don't know much of anything about you."

"There's not that much to know, trust me."

"Ever miss it, think about going back East?"

"To visit," I said.

"Not to live?"

"Not a chance."

"Really, you don't get homesick?"

"Not so much as I used to," I said. It was hard to explain. We were a close-knit family of mostly women. I never dreamed I'd live more than a few miles away. But then I left and discovered there was a whole big world out there, and it was mine if I wanted it. Sometimes, with all the time and distance, they felt like another lifetime.

"What about you?" I asked. "You never say anything about your life. What about your family?"

He examined his fingertips. "There were four of us, me, a sister, two brothers. My mother stayed home. She was a beautiful woman. Impeccably dressed—gloves, hats, high heels. My father traveled. Prep school for the kids. Weekends at the country club. You know..."

"I know?" I laughed. "Oh Ren, you snob, the closest I ever got to the country club was when we picked my mother up after her waitressing shift Friday nights at a place called the Green Valley Riding Club. That's probably where I'd be today if I hadn't gotten out of there."

"I don't believe that for a minute."

"There's nothing wrong with waitressing, Ren. You can make some decent money in tips."

"I'm sure you can," he said. "But you're smarter than that."

"It has nothing to do with smarts. It's what there was."

"You would have always found something more. I know."

"What about you?" I asked. "What did you do before you came here?"

"Oh, the usual. Nothing too exciting . . ." he said. He sipped his Scotch. "So, what else do you like to read, besides Fitzgerald?"

"You're changing the subject," I said.

"Poetry?"

"Some."

"How about Sylvia Plath? You like her?"

"Not particularly," I said.

"No?" He frowned. "How come?"

I thought for a moment.

"Too dark?" he asked.

"No, I just don't get the whole suicide thing," I said.

"What do you mean?"

"I think she was a coward."

"Pete. No, you can't mean that." He looked mildly dismayed as if I'd just made a joke in particularly bad taste.

"Of course, I can," I said.

"You don't understand. She wasn't a coward. Life is hard for some people. Too hard."

"That's no reason to kill yourself."

"And you would know?"

I nodded yes. But I had no idea what hard was. At least not the kind of hard Ren understood. I saw then that something had shifted, his sense of me had changed. "All I mean, Ren, is that life is short. You gotta live while you can."

Now he smiled again, one of those smiles that said he knew things I did not. One of those smiles that said he could forgive me my know-it-all-ness because I was young and knew nothing.

"There's a poem by Dorothy Parker, 'Resume,' that says something like that," he said. "Might as well live."

"See, now there's my kind of poet," I said.

"Oh Pete," he said shaking his head. "Dorothy Parker was a nasty drunk."

"But at least she didn't stick her head in a gas oven," I said.

"No, but maybe she should have," he smirked.

"Now who's being unkind?"

"Touché," he said, and reached across the table, just for an instant touching my hand. Our eyes met; I looked away.

"So, can I get you another glass of that or maybe something else, maybe some champagne in keeping with the spirit of our celebration?"

"Sure, why not?"

He disappeared and then returned with two flutes.

I took the glass from him and let the bubbles tickle my nose, then sipped.

He did the same. "Not bad for a cheap bubbly," he said, clinking his glass to mine. "Though there's no substitute for the real thing."

I wondered if I'd ever had the real thing, and if so, would I even know the difference.

"Have you been to France?" he asked.

"Me? Are you kidding? I don't even own a passport."

"Oh, you should. Really. Everyone needs to see Paris at least once."

He began to tell me why. But I had never been anywhere, and sitting there with him, listening to him talk about the Seine, Notre Dame, the Louvre, I again felt the expanse of my ignorance. I tried to think of something interesting, some place I had gone, or at least knew, but came up embarrassingly short. And then I remembered something I'd heard. "Do you know there's a place in Alaska where, when it freezes, you can walk across the ice to Russia?"

He paused and then broke into a big smile. "Apropos of?"

I felt my cheeks warm. Sometimes I said the stupidest things.

"Oh no," he reached for my hand, and squeezed it. "I'm sorry. And really, no, I didn't know that. Have you been there?"

I shook my head. "I don't even know if it's true, it's just what I've heard. I've never been anywhere, really. New Jersey and Alaska."

"That's more than some people, Pete." He looked at me, held my eyes until I had to look away, and then he said something, soft, so I could barely make it out at first.

"I knew a woman, lovely in her bones, / When small birds sighed, she would sigh back at them."

That was the first time I heard, really heard, his voice. It was like a melody, a song.

"Theodore Roethke," he said.

I nodded as if I knew. "You know," I said, "maybe I will bum a smoke. Just one."

That night, I dreamt I was on a mountain, fighting my way through thigh-deep powder toward the top. There was such a long way to go, I didn't know how I'd ever make it. Then came a crack. A gunshot, I thought. But no. Not a gunshot, an . . . The avalanche swept me off my feet and I was tumbling, tumbling, then suddenly still, suffocating under the weight of the snow, like wet concrete, forcing the life out of me. *Swim, Nate said. Swim.* I awoke, my arms clawing at the air, heart pounding, out of breath.

A second crack broke the early morning. Awake, I recognized the sound of snow breaking free from the roof and exploding onto the ground. Still my heart pounded.

FOUR

Valentine's Day came, and nothing from Nate. All day I waited, thinking any moment the flowers would arrive. They never did.

I was closing things up for the day, feeling sorry for myself and the solitary Valentine's evening ahead.

Denny stepped from the production room where Jeremy was coaching Di on a voiceover for a Wrassell Mall spot, and walked to my desk.

"You hear her lately?" he asked, tipping his head in her direction.

I nodded. This was shaky ground. If I said she was doing better, I'd be acknowledging she hadn't been very good. If I didn't say as much, it denied her improvement. I was trying to figure out the lesser of two evils.

"She's doing great, isn't she?" he said, solving my problem.

"She is," I agreed.

"I've been working with her at home. Jer's working with her here. It's paying off. Eventually, I want to sit down with you and start getting you ready for the TV gig."

"Cool," I said, though the idea of TV scared me speechless.

"Good. Listen, I'm headed over to Annie's to set up for the Valentine's party tonight," he said. "Di and Jeremy are right behind me. Come join us when you finish up."

"I'll probably just go home," I said.

"What's the matter, fly boy forget your flowers?"

I shrugged.

"It happens, kid," Denny said. "Between you and me, I damned near forgot myself. I really would have been in the doghouse then. Hell, she still hasn't forgiven me for that business with those brats of hers going home early at Christmas."

He drew on his cigarette, exhaling a stream in the direction of Di's desk. "You see those?" he asked, pointing his cigarette at a bouquet of miniature roses, three each of yellow, pink, lavender, peach, and ivory.

"She figure out who sent them yet?" I asked.

"No idea. I just hope to hell she hasn't attracted some weirdo. We've been getting hang ups at the house now. She tell you?"

"No. That's creepy."

He shrugged. "Di says I worry too much. It's probably nothing."

I followed him down the stairs and to the Scout. I'd had a new battery put in, but every time I went to start her up, I always wondered. I goosed the gas pedal a couple of times, and she turned right over. I jumped out to pull the plug. Up above, the window creaked open, and Mitch popped his head out. "Hey, Pete, hurry up. Your old man's on the phone."

I raced up the stairs, grabbing the phone as I rounded the front desk.

"Nate?"

"Hey, Babe, Happy Valentine's Day."

"I thought you forgot," I said.

"Forget? Are you kidding."

"No," I said in a voice suddenly gone warbly.

"Sweetheart, are you crying?"

"No."

"Are you sure?"

"Yes."

"Oh, Blondie, I'm sorry. You know me, I never remember these things on time. It's not that I don't think about you, believe me. It's just been one of those weeks."

"It's OK," I said. "I just miss you, Nate."

"I know. I miss you, too, Babe. But hey, maybe I can make it up to you."

"You think so?" I said.

"You can tell me how when you pick me up at the airport."

When we hung up a few moments later, I thought I knew just how people felt when they won the lottery. Nate was coming home. One whole week. I'd have taken an hour.

The bells on the door downstairs jingled and seconds later Ren was standing in front of my desk.

"Happy Valentine's Day, Patrice," he said.

"Happy Valentine's Day yourself, Reynolds."

He brought his hand from behind his back and held out a heart-shaped box covered in red cushiony cloth with a ruffle of ribbon in the center.

"For me? Ren, how sweet."

"I hope you like truffles," he said.

"Truffles? Wow." The hearts I knew came with various milk chocolates filled with sickly pink and white crèmes and the occasional peanut butter or nougat. If it was a really good one, it would sometimes have a few wrapped pieces, too. But truffles? No, we did not get hearts with truffles, and I was pretty sure he didn't find something like that on the bay.

I stood and leaned across the desk and kissed his cheek. "You're a sweetheart."

He started to say something, but the words got caught in his throat.

"Ren, you're blushing."

"I am? Really?" he said, that shy grin dimpling his cheeks. "So," he exhaled, "I ran into Denny. He said you were having a bad day."

"Not any more. Nate's coming home. In two weeks. Finally."

"Nate? Your husband." He brought his hand to his mouth and coughed. "How nice for you."

"I am so excited. It's already been over a month. And hey, maybe you'll finally get to meet him. You'll like Nate. Everyone does."

"Sure," he said.

"Hey, you going over to Annie's?"

"Actually, probably not."

"Come on, Ren, why not? Or, does someone have a hot date tonight?"

He frowned and shook his head. I wondered if he knew I was only teasing. But then he said he had to go and just like that he was gone again, leaving me to wonder, as I inhaled the bittersweet scent of a dozen perfect dark truffles, what I had missed.

It was a bitterly cold night, the kind where your first couple of breaths bruise your lungs and crinkle the inside of your nose. I looked to the sky for the northern lights, which had been out in greens and reds the last couple of nights, but just then, there were only the stars, like glitter on velvet.

Wrassell Annie's sat a couple of blocks down from KWLD. It was a long log building with a covered walkway skirting its front and a heavy single front door.

I tugged the door open. It was no fancy place. The exposed log walls inside were dotted with the things people—mostly summer visitors—left behind. Who knew why? Maybe to say they'd been there, too. Maybe to stake some small claim on a piece of Alaska before returning to their civilized lives. There were Polaroids stuck with pushpins, license plates, bumper stickers: "Move the Capital to Willow," dried flowers, a funeral card, rosary beads.

During the winter, it was just us locals, and we were happy to have Annie's to ourselves. In the summer, the patio was open and we all stayed outside, sometimes straight through the 1:00 a.m. dusk and right into sunrise again.

That night, Denny and the crowd occupied the usual tables all pushed together, chairs squeezed in so that everyone fit. I crunched across the peanut shells covering the old wood floor and took an empty seat at the scarred wood table next to Di.

"Pete, you changed your mind," Denny said from his spot at the head of the table. The barmaid brought me a white zin, and I told them my news.

"Hear, hear," Jeremy called, raising his glass. "To our lovely Pete, who is finally going to get a poke. Cheers." And we all—except Kyle and Skye, who were too intent on staring into each other's eyes to notice—clinked glasses in the center of the table.

The door opened and in walked Annie and Jack, looking like Alaska royalty in matching parkas trimmed in fur. Half the bar called out to greet them. Denny jumped to his feet and began directing us to make room for the pair while he found extra chairs. The two of them squeezed in at the end of the table. Denny beamed, proud to have the owners pick his table to join.

"Holy Jesus, Mary, and Joseph," Denny shouted. "Someone get me my sunglasses. What did you do, mug Liz Taylor?" We all turned to see what the fuss was about as a blushing Annie held up her hand. A diamond the size of a small nut caught the barroom light and sent it dancing in prisms across the room. A collective Oooooo went up from the bar, signaling a mix of surprise, envy, and no doubt a few broken hearts.

Jack, a quiet man whose emotions played out largely in the smile lines around his mouth and the wrinkles in the leathery skin by his eyes, watched our response, a humble but proud smile aimed at a his bride-to-be.

I looked down at the simple gold band on my hand. Someday. But just then I didn't care what kind of ring I wore, didn't care if I had any ring at all. Nate was coming home. God, I was happy.

"Let's see," Di said.

Annie slid her hand over to Di so she could get a closer look. Di's eyes widened. "Sheesh, Annabelle, that's some rock."

"Great Jack, now you did it," Denny said.

Jack twirled the silvery end of his mustache. "A pretty girl deserves a new bauble from time to time," he said, winking in Di's direction. "Especially one who would put up with you."

Di rolled her eyes. "When is the last time I said a word about a diamond, Den?"

"Let's see," Denny said, pretending to calculate.

"If I want good jewelry, dear, I'm perfectly capable of buying it myself," Di said.

"What do you mean, good?" Denny said, looking mildly insulted. "This isn't good?" He lifted her hand with the gold nugget and diamond band on it. "I thought you loved this ring?"

"Never mind," she said.

"Dames," Denny said to the rest of the table. Then to Di, loud enough for us all to hear, "All right, all right. You want a bigger diamond, doll. We'll get you a big diamond. A rock." He turned and winked in our direction.

Denny was broadcasting live from the tavern that night, and the next time he took the mic, Annie summoned him to give her a few minutes. As it turned out she wasn't finished with the surprises.

"Yes, it's true, Jack wants to make an honest girl of me and I said yes," she said, holding up her hand again. She waited out the applause and cheering.

"There's one other bit of news. Looks like our family is going to be growing. Jack has decided to get back in the race. The first batch of pups for the new sled dog team is on their way." She raised her mug, "To the Iditarod."

The bar went nuts again with cheers and slaps on the back. Jack had been a big musher in his day and having him in Wrassell was akin to having a NFL quarterback in our ranks. It was like we were already almost famous.

Denny took the mic back.

"All right everybody, this one is going out to Annie and Jack." And when "Going to the Chapel," came over the speakers, we all sang along to the very end—which happened to come right about the time the front door opened, letting in a blast of cold. A chubby woman with frizzy, rust-colored hair and a frazzled expression stood in the doorway, her hand clutching the tiny hand of a little girl, who held a red heart balloon on a string, their eyes adjusting to the light.

"Oh my God. Helen," Kyle said. And then again, "Helen," as he jumped to his feet, sending his chair crashing to the floor.

"Who?" Skye asked in a way that suggested she knew perfectly well who.

"It's you. You're here. Oh my gosh, what a surprise," Kyle said, now hurrying across the room to meet them.

Skye turned to me, "Did he say Helen?"

"I think so."

We watched the reunion from across the room: Kyle hoisting his daughter up on his hip, Helen smiling now, hand calming down the poufs of hair that sprouted out of place.

"Just what I need," Denny said.

Annie leaned across the table to me. "Who is that?"

"His wife," I said. "I think."

Skye just sat there, deer in the headlights, then excused herself to go to the ladies' room.

"Did she know he was married?" Annie asked.

"Sure she did," Denny said. "Until lately, he's been mooning around for his family back home like some lovesick teen. But you know what they say," he leaned in closer so we all could hear. "Absence makes the heart go wander."

"Oh Denny, that is not . . ." Annie said, eyes traveling to the bar. "Wonder what that's about?"

A cop stood by the bar, talking to the bartender.

Annie stood and made her way over.

We watched Annie and the officer until she made her way back to us.

"Damnedest thing. Ren Kennedy's missing."

"Missing?" I said. "How can that be? I just saw him."

"What do you mean, missing?" Di asked.

"They found his car parked out by a trailhead in the state forest," Annie said. "A ranger saw him start off down the trail earlier. Figures he'd gone out to get a better look at the northern lights away from the glare in town. Now they're worried he got himself lost out there."

I stayed awake most of that night worrying about Ren. He wasn't the kind to go off walking in the woods. He was never dressed for the Alaska winter. And he was surely no outdoorsman. He wouldn't know to build a snow cave, or where to search for dry kindling or pinecones to start a fire. What he didn't know could easily kill him before we got through the night.

The sky was just turning from dark to dawn when I pulled into the parking lot at the trailhead.

Spread before me was an expanse of towering, skinny evergreens, boughs weighted with snow, the white earth below pocked with pinecones and animal tracks. A man could wander in that forest for days, even weeks, and never be seen. In a state one-third the size of the Lower 48, and most of it wild, people went missing all the time. And this was how it happened. You took a wrong turn. Wandered off the path. Fell through thin ice. Slipped off an edge. Never to be heard from again. Oh Ren. I felt my eyes fill.

There were only a few trucks and cars in the parking lot. I climbed from the Scout and approached a ranger. Someone called my name.

I turned. There was Kate Brady, cup of coffee in one hand, her tape recorder slung over the opposite shoulder. She wore black slacks, little black flat boots with a fur ruff, and a down coat belted at the waist but open at the neck and damn if she wasn't wearing those pearls.

I wiped at my eyes and took a deep breath.

"You OK?" she asked, frowning.

"Fine. I've just got a cold." Seeing her all equipped and ready for duty, I realized with a novice's shame that I hadn't even thought about a story. "You're out and about early," I said.

"No kidding. Trust me, it's not by choice. Uncle Chris wants me to interview the search-and-rescue guys. Says they never get enough credit."

"You hear anything?" I asked.

"You mean about this Kennedy guy? Well yeah, they found him. Couple of hours ago. Your boss didn't tell you? Denny's over at Annie's with half the rest of the town."

"Is Ren OK?"

She shrugged. "I think so. I mean I'm sure he's got some hypothermia, maybe frostbite, that kind of thing. You know him or something?"

"He fills in at the station when we're short."

"That's right. I knew that. It seems kind of weird though. He didn't strike me as the outdoors kind."

"I know. He's not."

"So what, does he have a death wish or something? I mean who in their right mind goes off in the woods at night like that?"

I found Ren in hospital room 236, staring out the window, looking lost, looking like he wasn't really there.

"Ren?"

He turned to me with a look like he had just woken up.

"Pete," he said, managing a small smile.

"Oh Ren," I said, and then without thinking, hurried over and hugged him. "You had me scared half to death."

"I'm sorry about that," he said, taking my hand.

"Jesus, I'm glad you're OK."

"Here," he said, moving over to make room for me. I sat next to him.

"I'm glad you're here," he said.

I nodded, feeling shy suddenly.

"It was a stupid thing," he said. "I can imagine the talk around town."

"No, everyone's just glad you're OK."

He sighed and smiled a little half smile. "Oh, I'm sure there are a few jokes flying around about dumb cheechakos," he said. "But it's OK. I suppose I deserve them."

"No you don't. Well, then again . . ."

"Thanks," he said. I gave his hand a squeeze and winked.

"You know," he said, "it doesn't look like I'm going to stick around much longer. Before I go, you ought to come by the inn sometime and see the old place. I think you'd like it."

"So, you really are leaving," I said.

This time, he squeezed my hand and winked. "So, is that a yes?"

"Sure," I said. "But what's your hurry. We small town hicks boring you?"

"No, don't say that. Not at all . . . It's just, well, you . . ."

In the time it took us to register the footsteps, she was in the doorway. Big smile turning to disappointment, the bouquet of flowers falling to her side.

"Belinda," he said.

I stood from the bed.

"How kind of you to come," he said. "And flowers."

She looked at him, eyes wide, lips quivering. And I knew she was crushed. With Ren she would always be crushed.

"Hey," I said, casual as a candy striper. "I was just leaving."

Ren looked at me, opened his mouth to say something, then stopped. It was too awkward.

"Thanks for stopping by," he said.

"Take care, Bud," I said, though I'd never called him anything like that. Bud. Buddy. Pal. Friend. I wished he wasn't leaving. I wished I'd heard what he was about to say.

I hurried down the hall to the elevator. The doors were just closing and a nurse reached out to stop them. I stepped inside and she and another nurse resumed their conversation. Someone had been attacked by a grizzly. I half listened, but my mind was still back with Ren. The elevator dinged our arrival, the doors sprang open, and I walked to the Scout. I was halfway out of the lot when it registered. Minutes later, I was back with the recorder and notepad.

The first time I walked into a hospital looking for the survivor of a capsizing I learned that you never tell a hospital receptionist you're a reporter because right off they will make you sit and wait for the public relations person or some other administrative type. And meanwhile, the competition is figuring out the story.

But sometimes luck is on your side. Sometimes you walk onto the scene and everything clicks, the right people, the right questions, and you sit down to write, and the story pours straight off your fingertips.

And so it was that day. I strode past the front desk, and then the framed Polaroids of ER visitors snagged by fishhooks. In one, a treble hook was stuck just below the thumb; in another, a thick barbed hook was stuck through a swollen lower lip; and in a third, a woman's mouth gaped open to reveal the hook that had pierced her cheek. The elevator doors opened and once again carried me to the second floor hall.

I peeked into three rooms before I poked my head around the door of 212 and saw a dark haired guy not far from my age, arm in a sling, bandage around his head, a line of black stitches trailing one cheek.

I took a step inside and offered a tentative "Hi."

"Hi," he said. "It's OK, come on in."

"Are you the guy that . . ."

"Tangled with the griz?" he finished for me. "That's me, all right. Ronnie Johnson."

"I'm Pete. Pete Nash, with KWLD," I said, holding up the mic.

"Television?" he asked.

"No, sorry. Radio."

"That's OK. Radio is good."

I walked over to the bed to shake his hand.

"Wow, looks like you're lucky to be alive," I said.

"Tell me."

"Think I could run a tape and we could talk about what happened?"

"Sure, but I've never done this before," he said.

"Not to worry. Until recently, neither had I."

"You know," he said, "I was just laying here thinking this is just the kind of story you hear about on the news. One of those too-strange-to-be-true things."

He put his hand up to his head, touching lightly at the bandage, as if testing for pain.

"I was just skiing along, minding my own business. I rounded the corner and there she was. I don't know why she wasn't hibernating. Maybe she was sick. Maybe she hadn't gotten enough to eat in the summer. All I know is one minute I was trying to get turned around to get the hell out of there, and the next I was on the ground, blood running all over my face. You ever smell a bear up close?"

I shook my head.

"Like death. Decay. You smell that and instantly you're a believer, praying like you've been on your knees your whole life." He paused and took a deep breath.

"I knew if I tried to run, she'd kill me for sure. So I just rolled myself into a ball like they tell you and tried to protect my head. She bit at my shoulder and my back," he said, running his hand along a spot just below his ribs. "By then, I was pretty sure I was going to die, and I was just praying it would be fast. Then, just like that, she left me alone. I waited and waited. I was afraid to even breathe. I knew the minute I moved, she'd be on me. It seemed like forever. But then I lifted my head and looked around and she was gone. That's when I felt my head and realized half my scalp . . ." He shook his head. "Fuck." And then, "Sorry, can't say that on the radio, I know."

"It's OK," I said. "I can edit it."

"You know what's really weird? Aside from the fact that every other bear in Alaska is hibernating? Here's the really weird thing. The doctors said probably the only reason I was able to ski out for help was because I was stoned and so I was, like, you know, able to cope. If I'd been straight, I might have panicked and bled to death."

He blew his nose. "No shit, tell that to the anti-drug people."

It was a good story, but whether or not the AN would take it depended on what else was going on that day and who was on the desk. By the time the editor answered the phone I was already chiding myself for thinking I'd stumbled on to something big. It was Alaska. These things happened, and this guy hadn't even died. I was midway through the story, rushing to get in the most drama before he could say no, when he interrupted, "Go ahead, give me what you have."

I read; he typed. When I finished there was silence and finally, "No shit. The guy's stoned, gets attacked by a bear, flips his scalp back on, and skis seven miles for help?"

"And waves down a truck driver on the highway," I added.

"Jesus. Just when you think you've heard it all. Good job, Pete."

I wrote up three more versions of the story and dubbed three carts of sound so I could rotate them Monday morning. It *was* a good story, and all on tape, though I had to edit out the F-word. It was OK to smoke pot in Alaska, but you couldn't say *fuck* on the air.

FIVE

My bear story got some good play and attracted a couple calls from TV and the magazine *Outside*. I started dreaming maybe I had a chance at another best of the month. Then the serial killer story broke in the Anchorage newspapers, front page, top of the fold, the picture showing an ugly, skinny bespectacled man. The man who raped, abused, tormented, and ultimately murdered the women he deemed bad girls. Robert Hansen. He was an acne-scarred little man, a baker, a hunter, a pilot, father and husband, the killer, by his own account, of seventeen young women. He bound them with snare wires, blindfolded them with Ace bandages, hunted them when they ran. Then tossed their bodies in shallow graves.

The rumors had been true.

I wondered what Bobbie would have to say about the whole thing, but I wasn't walking back inside that strip joint to find out.

The day Nate was due in, I awoke to a morning sky the color of coffee with cream, with specks of ash floating in the dawn. It was not the usual chimney soot, but I had no idea what else it could be.

Halfway to work, Jeremy came out of a song, announcing "Stay with me, folks. I'll be right back to let those of you still snuggled in your beds know what you're in for when you rise, but if I were you, I would be in no hurry to climb out of the sack. Not today." He cut to a Wings 'N Things spot.

What the hell? I thought there must have been a fire, and I was hoping it wasn't bad, but even if it was, I didn't care. My husband was coming home. It was no day for breaking news.

Finally, Jeremy was back. "Well folks, according to NOAA, that's the National Oceanic and Atmospheric Administration to you, Mount Ivanof has erupted. That's the bad news. The good news is that, other than a little air pollution, it's probably not any cause for concern. Mount Ivanof is miles away, clear across the inlet. So no, this is not Bidarkee Bay's day to reenact Pompeii. Rise and shine. We're coming back at you at the top of the hour with Pete Nash and more information. Now, the Box Tops."

I exhaled. It was only a volcano.

I got to the newsroom and wrote up a few stories, including reminders to people with breathing problems to stay inside until the ash subsided. In between newscasts I paced, unable to concentrate on anything, crazy with the anticipation of seeing Nate.

Just after 9:00, he called.

"Hey, Babe, where're you at?" I said.

He sighed. I could probably count on one hand the number of times I'd heard Nate sigh. Nate was not a sigher. "At camp," he said.

"But Nate, I thought you were leaving at . . ."

"They grounded our flight."

"What do you mean? Who? Why?"

"It's the volcano, Babe. The ash clogs the engines."

"But it'll go away, won't it?"

"Eventually."

"Nate?"

"I'll call as soon as I know something."

One day passed, then two, and Mount Ivanof kept rumbling. By day three, when it blew again big time, we knew. Nate wasn't coming home. We said maybe later, but I knew. It was going to be a long damned spring.

"Hey Pete," Denny said, marching into my office. "I need you to do me a favor."

"Sure, what?"

"I want you to keep an eye on the scanner."

"What's going on?"

"Well, turns out you're not the only one crying in her beer this week. Helen's gone and run off and left some sort of good-bye-cruel-world kind a note, and Kyle's afraid she's going to do something stupid."

"He must have told her," I said. "Kyle told Skye he was going to ask for a divorce."

"Well, I guess Kyle has his answer. The little wife ain't gonna go quietly. I want you to keep an ear on that thing just in case she does do something idiotic."

That weekend, while I sat at home drinking too much white zin from the box and feeling sorry for myself, word was spreading of Helen's craziness. She had not killed herself, but she had managed to roll their Pinto wagon on a patch of black ice on a shaded curve, earning herself a sprained wrist and a few scrapes and bruises.

We heard all about it Monday morning, but it wasn't until a few hours into the day that we realized what it really meant.

I was on the air when Lydia came flying up the stairs, looking like a woman about to spontaneously combust. Jeremy saw her, too and turned to me, eyebrows raised. Lydia blew into Denny's office. Denny stood from his desk, and immediately moved to shut the door.

I hurried through the news, skipping sports and business and going straight to the weather. I just wanted to see what the hell was going to happen with Lydia.

It was only minutes before she came waltzing out of the office, Denny right behind her with that pleading look you hated to see on anyone's face. She turned to him, finger wagging, head shaking, black hair swinging in emphasis. I signed off. Denny came back up the stairs, looking defeated. Jeremy keyed up a song, then went to Denny.

Moments later, Denny locked up his office and left. I knew he was going to drown his sorrows, whatever they were, at Annie's. I slipped into the studio where Jeremy stood, hands on hips, staring off into space. "What's going on?" I asked.

"Pete, old girl. I believe you have just witnessed the beginning of the end."

"The end? Of what?"

"Lydia pulled her ads."

"No."

"Yup. We are officially screwed."

"We have others."

"Oh Pete, puhlease. You do traffic. You see. What do we have? A bunch of PSAs and those little fifteen- and thirty-second spots Denny has been nearly giving away? Those won't even cover payroll. And on top of it, George just summoned Denny to Anchorage."

I felt that sick sort of roller-coaster drop in my stomach. George was our investor. The man who'd made KWLD possible. I'd met him only once, but I talked to him on the phone from time to time. He was a bearded old guy, with long white hair, who favored flannel shirts and old style dungarees with suspenders. I sensed early on that he regretted pairing up with Denny. He was a self-made millionaire, a no-nonsense, no-bullshit kind of guy. And Denny was as full of it as they came. Last couple of times he'd called, Denny hadn't been around and I could tell George wasn't happy.

"But I don't understand," I said. "Why did Lydia pull her ads? She's always been with us, the car lot and the mall."

He crossed his arms over his chest and leaned back against the counter, then sighed. "Because it seems Kyle and Helen and Skye have confused life with a country-western song. Sunday morning, bruised and bandaged, with the little munchkin close at hand, Helen showed up at Lydia's church."

"Oh shit," I said.

"Oh, that's not the half of it," Jeremy said, eyebrows raised, a wry smile skewing his mouth. "The part where they ask for prayers and concerns?"

"Yeah."

"That's when Helen stood, recounted for one and all her troubles, and asked, no doubt in a tremulous voice, for prayers to save her little family. I'm told it was very moving indeed."

"Wow."

"You got it. So there, Pete, is your answer to why we are now not merely inching toward oblivion, but rocketing at Mach one for it."

I never knew for sure how it went—if Kyle decided on his own to leave or if Denny didn't give him any choice—but a couple of days later, he shuffled into the newsroom to let me know he was taking the wife and kid back home to the Midwest.

"For good?" I asked.

"Helen thinks so," and then he brought a finger to his lips.

I nodded.

"I just need to get some things settled, save some money," he said. "It's easier to get ahead back there and not nearly so cold."

"And your wife won't run into your girlfriend every other day," I said.

He drooped further and gave me that wounded look. "I'm sorry," I said. "Just trying to get a laugh out of you." I stood and walked over to hug him. "I'll miss you."

"Take care of Skye for me 'til I get back, huh?"

I nodded.

"I will be back," he said, his voice all dramatic whisper, his fist clenched.

"We'll be here," I said. Wouldn't we?

SIX

Driving in to work, I popped out the Journey cassette, and tuned in to KWLD. Jeremy usually did a quick update on the world at large until I got there to do my first newscast, and it gave me an idea of what kind of morning I was in for.

Except this morning Jeremy wasn't on the air. Mitch was. What the hell? Mitch was evenings. Where was Jeremy? And please, someone, tell me he didn't quit. Jeremy pissed me off regularly, but I'd never deny how much we needed him.

I pulled into the parking lot at the station and ran up the stairs, but the studio door was closed; the red light above it glowing. I went to the newsroom and watched Mitch through the window. He turned to me. I flipped my palms open. He held up a finger, finished his bit, hit play, and closed the mic. We met between the studio and newsroom.

"Where's Jeremy?" I asked.

"What, too good to work with the evening drive jock?"

"Seriously," I said. "Do you have to be such a dick?"

"Jeez, someone woke up on the wrong side. Jer's sick. Di called and asked me to fill in."

"What's wrong with him?"

"Beats me, just some bug, I guess. Hope the hell I don't catch it."

"What about your shift?"

"Di said she's got it all taken care of."

"She was here already?"

"No, she called. She had to take Denny to the airport to catch his plane. She'll be in later."

Di was no fashion plate, but that morning she showed up looking like she was vying for the crown of Mrs. Bidarkee Bay, which was in fact a bona fide part of the Mrs. Alaska pageant circuit. She wore a beige suede suit with matching knee-high boots and a ruffled blouse. She had little dangly pearls in her ears, and she'd taken extra care with the hot rollers that morning.

"Look at you," I said. "New?"

"Actually, old," she said. "I just never go anywhere to wear it."

"Very nice," I said. "Special occasion?"

She rolled her eyes. "I wish. Sales calls. Denny's all wigged out about losing Lydia, and I figured, you know, what the hell, a little extra oomph can't hurt. Besides, I get sick of the same old pants and boots and dowdy Michelin Tire coat."

"Believe me, I know," I said. "I can't even tell you the last time I put on a dress. Denny's plane get off OK?"

"Fine. On time, even. I don't know what he's going to tell George, though. He better think of something." She checked her reflection in the newsroom window, fluffed up her hair, and pulled out a tube of lipstick.

"Listen, I gotta run," she said, watching her reflection in the window to freshen the pink color on her lips. She wound the color back into the tube, snapped on the lid, and dropped it in her purse. "I've got a busy day, so I doubt I'll be back until later this afternoon after I pick up Denny."

But that's not the way it went. Four hours later, I picked up the phone and there was Denny looking for a ride. He'd come in early. I found him sitting in the airport bar, working on a tumbler of whiskey.

"No Di?" he asked.

I shook my head no. "She said she'd be out most of the day."

"Hmph. All day?" He frowned into his whiskey glass. Then shrugged. "That's right, today's Rotary, and I guess she did have some sales calls lined up."

He emptied his glass and signaled to the barmaid. "You want something?" he asked.

"A Diet Pepsi would be good," I said, sliding onto the stool next to him.

The barmaid filled his glass and slid the soda to me. I made a survey of the dead heads on the wall: moose, caribou, goat. There was a full brown bear in attack mode in one corner and a mammoth King Salmon mounted over the jukebox. I fished in my purse for change and walked over and played a couple of songs.

"Jesus, Pete, couldn't you have at least played something decent," he said.

"What? I like Prince."

"I like Prince," he mimicked. Then, "It's shit. It's not music, it's shit."

"Sorry," I said.

He tipped his head as if to say I was excused if only because I was too stupid to know any better. Then, "So, you'll be happy to know we are finished with George."

"We are?"

"We are." He took a sip of whiskey, lowered the glass, and turned to me. "And what are you looking so glum about?" He held the glass in midair, awaiting my answer.

"Nothing. Not glum," I said, faking a smile.

"It doesn't have to be a huge deal, Pete. There are other investors. George isn't the only man in Alaska with money. And the really good news is, it means I don't have to take any more of his shit."

I just sat there nodding, wondering what the hell we were going to do now.

"Listen, kid, all we gotta do is get through breakup. Once summer is here, we'll be fine."

He was right. Mostly. Once the tourists came, once fishing season started, once people got outside and started spending money, we probably would be OK. Except, there would always come that day again when the termination dust appeared on the mountaintops and the days grew shorter. And there we'd be all over again.

"Here's what I've figured so far," Denny said. "We'll start signing off the air at midnight. Nobody listens then, anyway. And obviously there's not going to be any raises. And no more trades. The staff wants something from Wings 'N Things, you're going to have to pay for it yourselves.

"And I'm thinking it's time for an Elvis revue. High time. Maybe we'll make it a fund-raiser. Something for those dames over at that crisis center place or maybe the animal shelter. That's how I met Di. You know that?"

"Uh-huh," I said. Everyone knew that.

"Yep, old theater on Fourth Avenue. She was right there in the front row with a bunch of her girlfriends . . . caught my eye and pffffttt, I was a gone guy."

I smiled. I'd heard the story a hundred times. We all had, but Denny loved telling it.

He sighed. "I'll probably have to get her to take the seams out on the jumpsuit," he said, patting his gut. "Yeah, I know I'm getting fat. But thank God for that little lady, don't know what I'd do without her."

I raised my Diet Pepsi in agreement, and we clinked our glasses and sipped.

"But see, now here's the tough part."

I turned to him.

"I've tried my damnedest to avoid this, but there's just no getting around it. She's going to have to get a job."

"A job? Outside the station, you mean?"

"Well shit, Pete. You think I don't feel bad enough? But you see the log books. When's the last time she sold anything?"

I shrugged.

"Exactly. Aside from the dribs and drabs here and there, she hasn't. Never has. I love the woman dearly, but she's just not cut out for sales. I'll still get her into the studio to help out with some of the spots. But the truth is—and this doesn't go any further—we're barely paying our own bills. We need another paycheck, a real paycheck."

"Does she know?"

"Not yet. It's something I've been thinking about for a while now. But I wanted to be ready." He reached inside his leather jacket and pulled out a small velvet box. "What do you think?" He flipped open the lid to reveal a diamond the size of your average pearl.

"Wow," I said.

"Wow is right," he said. "I'll get you the paperwork for the Diamonds in the Wild spots later. And not a word to anyone."

"About the ring?" I asked.

"That it's a trade."

Ren strode into the station that afternoon looking healthy and rested, carrying a bag from Wings 'N Things. He was dressed a little differently than usual, jeans and brown suede hiking boots in place of the khakis and leather boots he usually wore. But still the wool jacket with the suede patches on the sleeves and still that crisp white oxford beneath.

I waited until Mitch signed off and Ren got settled in the studio, then walked the latest weather and sports over to him.

"Well hey, I was beginning to think you were going to ignore me all day," Ren said.

"I wasn't ignoring you," I said. "I was working."

"Really?" he said, fixing me with that sly half grin of his.

"Really," I said, unable to help grinning back at him. It was like some sort of code between us. For what I wasn't sure. "How are you?"

"I'm fine, thanks."

"You look good," I said, backing toward the door.

"Hey wait, where're you going already?"

"I should probably be up front watching the phones," I said.

"You can watch this phone," he said. "See, I'm watching it right now, and it hasn't run off yet."

I hesitated. He grabbed the stool they kept in the studio for the occasional guest, and set it next to him. "See," he said with a flourish of his hands. "Just for you."

The song ended. He flipped open the mic. "And that was The Happenings with 'See You in September.' Ah yes, saying good-bye at the station. I remember it well," he turned to me, smiling. "Now, Mr. Gene Pitney, 'Twenty-four Hours from Tulsa.'"

"Dearest, darling, I had to write to say that I won't be home anymore."

I walked to the stool and hitched myself up next to him. "Just for a second," I said.

"You're always running off on me. Here," he said, tucking a breaded piece of chicken heart between my lips, "a piece of my heart."

It was supposed to be funny, I knew. But I felt my cheeks grow warm and for a second I couldn't move, couldn't chew, couldn't swallow. The blinking line on the phone caught my attention and brought me back to earth, and with unsteady hands I pulled the headset over my ears and answered.

"Hey Pete, you hear anything from Di yet?"

"No, nothing yet."

"Well that's odd. She didn't make the chamber meeting, either. I just checked."

"Probably just got caught up with clients," I said.

"Well, when she shows up, tell her I'm over here at Annie's."

"What's up?" Ren asked when I hung up.

"Nothing really," I said. "Denny can't find Di."

"Is she lost?"

"She's just not where she's supposed to be, I guess."

"Wives tend to do that."

"And you would know?"

"I would indeed."

"You're married?" I said.

"Was," he said. "I've never shown you pictures of my girls?"

"I didn't even know you had kids."

"Shame on me." He reached inside his jacket and pulled a wallet from an inside pocket. "This is Genevieve. She's ten. She's very smart. She takes ballet and sings in the youth opera. And this is Angelique. She's eight. She plays piano and chess. A tomboy, that one."

"They're here in Alaska?"

"No," he said, sighing. "My ex has them in Boston."

I sensed we needed a happier subject. "By the way, nice boots."

"Really, you like them?"

"They look good. And the jeans. You're actually starting to look like you live in Alaska."

"Well gee, thanks," he said.

"Girlfriend pick them out?" I said, trying to play it light. I almost said Belinda, but that seemed unkind.

"My girlfriend?"

"Oh come on, Ren, don't play coy with me. I'll bet you have a half a dozen girlfriends around here."

He blushed. "No, really, I don't. It was just, I really hadn't brought much with me when I came, so I finally broke down and bought a few things."

"I don't believe you for a minute," I said. "I'll bet you take them all chicken hearts and woo them with promises of Paris."

"No Pete, really, I . . ."

We heard the tires crunch across the gravel and ice out front and leaned toward the window to look. "Denny. I better get out front," I said.

"Thanks for keeping me company," he said, adding, "Patrice." And then, just as easy as that, he leaned over and kissed me. And when he did it a second time, I kissed him back.

I met Denny out at my desk.

"Still no Di?" he asked.

I was trying to recover from Ren kissing me, and when I opened my mouth the words caught in my throat and came out all garbled.

"What are you all frazzled about?" he asked.

I shook my head. "Nothing, I had food in my mouth."

"Di was supposed to pick me up at the airport in a half an hour. If we don't hear from her by then, we're calling the cops. Seriously. I don't know what the hell to think."

"Did you check the house?" I asked.

"Do I look stupid, Pete?"

The door opened with a whoosh from below.

"Whew, what a day," we heard her say.

Denny exhaled, turned his eyes heavenward, then to me. "See what did I tell you? She's fine."

"Denny?" Di said, climbing the stairs. "What are you doing here? I thought I was picking you up at 5:00?"

"I got in early," he said, crossing his arms over his chest. "Where were you?"

"Where was I?" she said coolly, eyebrows raised. "I was out trying to sell ads. Isn't that where I was supposed to be?"

"Of course it is, dear," he said, his voice changing to the soothing tones used to smooth rumpled feathers. "But next time you're going to take off like that, check in once in a while, huh? Poor Pete here was worried sick."

That night as I waited for sleep, I heard the Mercedes turn in to the driveway and realized I'd been listening for him all along. I heard the car door open and softly close, then the light tapping on the window of the door.

I stared up at the open beams on the ceiling. On the center beam, in a place tucked up tight against the ceiling were our initials—mine and Nate's—and the date, carved there just before Nate guided the boom and lifted the beam into place. We couldn't see them once the cabin was finished, but we knew they were there. They would always be there.

Ren tapped again. "Pete," he said softly.

Everything in that cabin we'd scrimped for. Paydays, we'd buy one thing. The bathroom sink. A refrigerator, dented on the side and discounted. Likewise, the stove. The old black rocker/recliner, found at a garage sale, and like new. It had never made me feel poor, but oddly smart, as though we were paving our way to better things by making such choices now. That our day would come.

"Pete, it's me, Ren." He waited. I heard his footsteps on the porch and imagined him peering into the window.

The kiss at the radio station, it was not such a big thing. Kid stuff. But here, in the cabin, away from the world, no phones for an excuse, no boss on the way, not so much as a nosy neighbor to dodge . . . Then, he would be part of the cabin, too. And I would always know.

Another tap on the door, this time with conviction. "Pete? Come on, Pete, just for a minute?" I pulled the pillow over my head and didn't move until I heard the Mercedes engine turn over.

I thought it might be the most unkind thing I'd ever done. Or maybe the kindest. I thought if he had just knocked once more.

SEVEN

A month passed. Breakup grew closer. Di got a job at the Sears catalog shop. And we hung on, one song, one contract, one hope and prayer at a time. It was never clear if there would be money for payroll and sometimes there wasn't, but somehow Denny always came up with it sooner or later. We were playing out our days like the condemned. And yet. And yet. We were KWLD. We had fans. We had listeners. We had plans. Radio stations didn't just fade away, did they? I had never known one to. I had grown up listening to WFIL, a Philly station so popular they put out their own albums of summer hits, one I had even found all the way up north in Anchorage in a Pay 'n Save years after it had been released. I found it in the clearance rack with a red discount price, and it was like finding an old old friend in a foreign place. No, radio stations did not just go away and we wouldn't either. We couldn't.

"How's the log book looking," Denny asked, coming out of his office one afternoon after spending nearly the whole morning cooped up inside on the phone. "Everything caught up?" he asked.

"Yeah," I said. How could it not be, there was barely anything there.

"Good. I'm going to need it. I'm going out of town for a couple of days. I'll leave tomorrow afternoon. I want you to pack up the log books, the contract files, and bank books. And get me the commuter flight schedule."

He paused and picked a piece of tobacco from his tongue. "Oh, and I want you to post a note in the break room, staff meeting tomorrow at Annie's. Five o'clock. I'll be back later."

I slipped off early Friday so the cabin wouldn't get too cold if the meeting ran late. The temperatures had begun to warm some. They'd opened the highway over the pass just that morning, but the weather report was calling for snow and colder temperatures again. And I still worried about the pipes freezing. It was typical spring weather in Alaska. One minute you were pulling out your cutoffs, the next, shoveling snow.

At the cabin, I wadded up some newspaper and built my teepee, struck a match, and watched her catch. I had come to understand the art of fire building, how a big log set just so to the rear of the fire will reflect the heat outward, while the log itself slowly smolders, and how a good bed of coals properly fed will glow hot for hours on end. I had given up on Nate coming home for a weekend. The troubling part was, I didn't really mind. I had joked with him that I was getting so good at living alone I barely needed a man anymore. "Don't you go getting too good at it, Pete," he'd said. "I'm coming home one of these days."

We'd laughed, but the truth was, I couldn't say when the last time was that I'd caught an unexpected glimpse of his picture or the hint of his scent from a piece of clothing and felt the old longing that had once nearly taken my breath away. Nate had become a fond and powerful memory, a warm, familiar voice on the other end of the phone; and I had become a solitary woman, enjoying the freedom that came with being on my own.

I marked off another day on the calendar, adding one more X to the rows of red marks that filled most of January, all of February, March, and now into April. It was a good feeling to know I had come through all those winter days on my own and done just fine, hard to imagine I'd been so fearful of so much. When it came down to it, Alaska was just like any other place—fraught with a certain amount of danger, but most places were, just different kinds.

I smiled at the thought of that and laid the marker back in the countertop basket. That's when I sensed it, a presence, the feeling that I wasn't alone, like the universe had read my thoughts and was warning me, don't be getting too smug. I turned to the sliding glass door that lead to the back deck, and seeing him, gave a startled yell and jumped. It was a bull moose, damned near the size of a VW van with a rack on his head like a couple of ceiling fans, separated from me by what now seemed a very flimsy sheet of glass.

I stood, frozen in place, watching him with both awe and apprehension. He just stood there staring back, chewing his cud. Then, like a tourist who'd stopped to take in the view and found it only so-so, he turned away and meandered off back into the woods. Some people laughed about moose, called them big and dumb and slow. But I knew better. I had been on campus when a senior accounting major tried to sneak by a young bull and was trampled to death. It's not something you easily forget, and when I walked outside that afternoon for a load of wood, I took the .38 with me.

Denny and Cork were at our usual table in the back corner. Denny looked annoyed; Cork, who had taken over Kyle's midday shift, looked merely miserable.

"Didn't I say five o'clock?" Denny asked, gesturing to the clock that read 5:00 straight up.

"That's what I put in the note," I said, pulling out a chair opposite him.

The door swung open. Ren spotted us and grabbed the chair next to mine. I scooted over to make a little more space between us. I needed to keep some distance from him—while I still could.

"I'm not contagious, promise," he said.

"Just giving you a little room," I said.

"You busy tomorrow morning?" Denny asked Ren.

"Not that I know of," Ren said.

"Jeremy needs the morning off for a doctor's appointment. Mind covering for him?"

"Sure," Ren said.

"Ren's going to cover for you," Denny called to Jeremy when he pushed through the heavy wood front door seconds later.

"Good to know," Jeremy said. "Appreciate it, Ren."

Next came Di, a sleeping Billy hitched on her hip.

For an instant, Denny brightened. "Hey, you made it," he said. "I didn't expect you."

"You're welcome," she said. "I had to leave work early and then scramble to get him at the sitter's."

"You could have left him there a little longer," Denny said, pulling out a chair for her.

"I thought you might want to spend some time with him while I run some errands since you're going to be gone," Di said.

"Sweetie, it's only the weekend. The taxi is picking me up in a bit."

"Taxi?" she said.

"Cheaper than parking all weekend. Unless you want to take me."

"Sorry," she said. "I have things to do."

So she still hadn't forgiven him for the whole work thing. That's what I thought. And I thought if we could just get the station back on solid ground, they would work it out; they'd be OK. We were so close. Breakup was just around the corner, then summer.

Billy awoke, and finding himself in a strange place, let out a frightened cry.

"Ah, come here little one, come to your uncle Jer," Jeremy said, reaching across the table to Billy.

"You never learn, Jer," Denny said. "I'm telling you, this tyke's strictly his daddy's boy."

Billy reached his arms out for Jeremy, and Jeremy folded him against his chest.

Denny smiled a rueful smile, then dinged a spoon against his glass. We quieted.

"I called you all here because I have some news," he began. "I wish it were better. But it is what it is."

He paused, watching us.

Oh shit. Was this it? Where would I go? It wasn't like there were a dozen other radio stations I could apply at.

Denny continued. "This evening, I'm flying to Garnet." He paused, looking around the table, then, "Chris Cole is interested in buying KWLD."

Someone gasped, and it wasn't until Denny turned to me that I realized it was me.

"I know for some of you that feels like the ultimate betrayal," Denny said. "I know, they were our competitors. But I'm out of options. I'm hoping to stay on as manager. I'm also hoping this will save your jobs."

Di cleared her throat. "What does George say?" she asked.

"George has no say," he said.

"Isn't he still legally a partner?"

He frowned.

Something wasn't right. Didn't she know? Didn't they talk about these things at home?

"Chris can handle that," Denny said. "If and when the time comes."

Funny how quickly the worst possible news becomes maybe not so bad after all. Because even if we had to be owned by the Coles, not such bad people, really, at least there was a chance I would keep my job. At least for the time, I would be saved from fetching coffee for some big shot in a suit. That was my big dread. Office work.

"I'm curious," Jeremy said. "Why would Cole want to buy the station if it's doing so poorly?"

"Simple. Chris Cole recognizes we have a presence here and with two stations he can cut better deals than ever. He'll have no competition." He took a hit off his cigarette and exhaled out the corner of his mouth.

"Should be interesting," Di said, sighing. "But hey, I've got to scoot. I've got a bunch of errands to run."

"Remember, you've got an appointment at the brake shop," Denny said.

"It's on my list. Last thing I do today," Di said.

Denny nodded. "Thanks, Babe." And then to her retreating back, "Hey, you sure you don't want to come with me to Garnet."

She waved her fingers in the air behind her. "Bye," she called, then disappeared out the door with Billy.

It wasn't too much later that Jeremy said he was going to get, and I said I'd walk out with him. Ren caught my eye, but I glanced away because I knew he would try to communicate some wish for me to stick around. And I knew I would be tempted.

Outside, Jeremy turned to me. "So, Pete, the pass is open now, huh?"

"They opened the avalanche gates this morning."

"Does that mean they'll keep them open?"

"They'll try."

"What's that supposed to mean?"

"It's Alaska, Jer. Mother Nature doesn't always cooperate."

"Tell me about it."

In all that time since the sock hop, the Scout hadn't given me trouble, but that afternoon when I walked back to the station she refused to start. I was trying to figure out what to do next when I heard a car pull up behind me. "Not again," Denny said from the window of the Wrassell Cab.

"Again," I said.

"Sorry, kid, I'd give you a ride, but I've got a plane to catch." The taxi crept forward, then stopped. Denny leaned out. "Tell you what, go on and take the Suburban."

"Really?"

He shrugged and pulled a set of keys from his pocket.

"What the hell," he said. "Won't be mine much longer anyway. But hey, I want you to bring it back here in the morning first thing in case Di wants to use it while her car's in the shop, and don't go running all over creation."

"It's a deal," I said.

He made as though to toss the keys. I nodded I was ready. He launched them, and they sailed through the air, landing perfectly in my cupped hands as if we traded such passes every day. For a second we paused, me trying to figure a way to say thanks, thinking I should run over and hug him. Then the cab started creeping away. He raised his hand in a wave. And I did the same. I always wished I'd given him that hug.

I unlocked the Suburban and hoisted myself up. On the outside, the truck sported a custom paint job of a mountain, a stream, and some Alaska wildlife. Inside, the seats were black leather. It was a huge rig, bigger than anything I'd ever commandeered and I felt like a kid just learning to drive all over again.

Pulling out of the parking lot, I saw Jeremy on the opposite side of the highway. I tooted the horn and waved. He looked and smiled, then did a double take, and frowned. I guessed he was a little miffed that he was walking, and here I was driving the Suburban—THE Suburban.

I turned onto the highway and headed for home. I was just about a mile out of town when I saw the flash of red in the brush. A fire truck. I slowed to get a better look. There were no flames, just a faint whiff of smoke, and only that one truck so far as I could see. I thought about turning around and going back, but then I would have to leave Denny's rig on the shoulder and hike in through the snow, and I wasn't wearing boots, and it was nothing, anyway. I was sure. Probably a brush fire. Kids playing with matches. I kept going, debating all the way home whether to go back, but then I pulled into the driveway, and there he was, and I forgot all about it.

He was standing by the Mercedes, a sheepish look about him. I parked the Suburban and hopped down.

"Look at you," he said. "How'd you manage that?"

"Must be my charming personality."

"Indeed," he said, chuckling.

And then he grew serious. "I couldn't help noticing you seem kind of, I don't know . . . Have I done something to upset you?"

"No, not at all," I said.

"You just seem distant, I guess."

"Ren. I'm married."

He glanced up, met my eyes. "I know that."

"I'm sorry." And I was—for all kinds of things. That we could never be. That I was so close to betraying my husband. That it felt like my life was over and now it seemed I'd never taken the chance to even live it. Not like I should have. I wanted to shout to the missing Nate, "See, this is why you shouldn't have gone."

Instead, I just looked at Ren and thought how damned much I liked him. And how I could never let him know or I'd be done. He sighed. I looked away.

It had begun to snow.

"Come on," I said. "Before we both get wet."

"Thanks," he said, following me. "Hey, by the way, you really should lock your door."

"I know, I should." I told him about the moose. "I don't want to be standing here fiddling with keys if he shows up again."

Inside, I fed the woodstove. He watched from across the room, leaning against the breakfast bar.

"Pretty big bomb Denny dropped," he said. "You OK?"

"Guess I have to be. It's not like I can do anything about it."

"Well, at least maybe it'll be a way to save KWLD."

"I know, but it still feels like betrayal. I'll bet Kate Brady is loving it. My luck she'll end up being my boss," I said, latching the woodstove door and standing.

"You know, I don't know of too many other women who could have toughed out a whole winter here alone," he said. And then, laughing, "Actually, I don't know too many men, either."

"It's my home. Where else would I go?"

"I suppose that's one way to look at it," he said, crossing the room to me. He took my hands in his, watched me for a moment, then drew in closer. I dropped his hands and backed away.

"No, Ren. I mean it."

He nodded, and exhaled heavily. "All right then," he said more to himself than anything.

"We can be friends," I said. "But that's it."

"Fine, whatever you say. So come on, it's Friday. How about you let me show you around the inn, and then I'll take you for a bite to eat."

"No. I'm going to stay put."

"Oh come on, Pete. You'll love the place."

I shook my head, and fixed my eyes on a spot outside the window beyond him.

"Pete."

"No, Ren."

He shook his head. "You're tough, Pete. I'll give you that."

"No, not tough, just practical."

"Right," he said, backing to the door. "Practical."

"Hey, by the way," I said, "take the road. The lake's probably OK, but it's getting to be that time of year. I wouldn't trust it."

"I never have," he said. "I never have." And then he was gone.

I sat alone for a bit, thinking about Ren. Thinking about how much I'd come to like him and how I'd never seen it coming. This was how it happened. How people fell in love when they had no right doing so. I needed to knock it off and find a way back to reality.

I picked up a notepad and pen. I didn't even know the last time I'd written Nate. But then, he wasn't much for letters any more, either.

I sat in my chair by the stove and started.

Hey Babe, sorry it's been so long since my last letter. Things are pretty quiet.

And then I couldn't find another damned word to write. Oh, there was plenty of news. The moose, KWLD. Hell, once I could fill a couple of graphs just on the weather and my fire-building efforts alone. But my hand stayed frozen, until finally it began moving again. *Dear Nate, get your ass home before I do something really stupid.*

I dropped the pad and pen to the floor. Screw it.

I walked to the refrigerator. Shit. I had forgotten to get wine. And all I had for food was a stale loaf of bread, a couple of slices of cheese, and a handful of condiments. Surely, Denny would forgive me a quick trip to the grocery store.

Already I was getting used to the Suburban. My Scout was no little rig, but the Suburban dwarfed it, and aside from the comfort factor, there was a security to it. I wondered if we'd ever be able to afford something like it. Or, even if we could, if Nate would ever go for putting that kind of money into a car. Nate was funny about things like that. He didn't like to waste money on something that was going to depreciate anyway. I used to think it was a virtue, but now I didn't see the point. Why work so hard if you couldn't enjoy it?

I pulled into the Safeway parking lot as Skye was coming out. I honked. She looked up just as she was passing, her mouth opened when she saw it was me at the wheel. She hit the brakes and backed up next to me.

"Wow," she said. "Denny let take you that?"

"The Scout's dead."

"Bummer. Hey, Di find you?"

"No. I didn't know she was looking for me. Did she say what she wanted?"

Skye shook her hand. "Nah, she just asked if I'd seen you. She probably just wanted to make sure you knew about the body."

Mitch met me at the top of the stairs, wire copy in hand. "Thought you might be looking for this," he said, handing it to me. I read.

Wrassell—Breaking news, Kate Brady, KBAY. Dead Man Found in Burned Vehicle.

Firemen called to a brush fire Friday afternoon found a smoldering car and the body of a man inside. Police say it appeared the man had been shot.

Shit. Brady had beaten me in my own back yard and all because I'd been too lazy, too caught up in the soap opera that was becoming my life.

Minutes later an update from the AN printed out. "Shooting Victim Identified." His name was Adam Kurosawa. He was a transient, newly arrived in Alaska, with a record in various states of small-time crimes, mostly drugs. That, I figured, pretty much answered that.

I walked outside to a world turning slowly white. The parking lot at Annie's was empty, the highway empty.

I didn't think about where I was going, I just drove until I came to the docks and the two-story red-and-white building with the frosted windows and the faded wood sign that said Borealis Inn.

Icicles hung from the gutters in long silvery spikes, illuminated by the lanterns mounted below. For a moment, I considered turning around, but then there he was by the window, smiling like I had just made him the happiest man on earth. And for the first time I understood that he was already in love with me.

He crept out over the slick deck to meet me, and arm in arm, slipping, sliding, laughing, we crossed back over the ice. "Whew," one of us said, as though we had just crossed some treacherous great divide. And suddenly, I felt nervous and awkward, like it was a first date, like he was a stranger. Inside, he took my coat and squeezed my hands between his. "What is it that they say, cold hands, warm heart?"

I smiled and let him rub my hands.

"I blew it," I said.

"Oh no, what happened?" he asked, still holding my hands.

I told him the latest news.

"Hey, you can't break every story."

"But I could have had this one. I wasn't paying attention."

"Lots on your mind these days."

"If you only knew," I said.

He squeezed my hands. "Come on, I'll give you the tour."

He led me up a flight of wood stairs and down the narrow hall of empty rooms. His was at the end, furnished like a monk's: narrow bed, banker's lamp, dresser, and a small desk, empty save for a notepad, three freshly sharpened pencils, and a book by T. S. Eliot.

Back downstairs, he showed me the kitchen, still with the old commercial refrigerator and gas range, and then to the empty lounge, where a huge wooden bar with mirror and elaborate carvings sat still intact.

"This is where I spend most of my time," he said, stopping in the doorway of a small room with windows looking over the bay. "This was the library," he said, "the place everyone retired to after a day on the water to trade fish stories and smoke their cigars." He chuckled softly. "Somehow, I can't see me doing either," he said.

There was a single chair, low and wide and covered in dark red leather. Next to it sat a small, round marble-topped table and stained glass lamp, and on the floor, a rug, nearly the size of the room, a patchwork of tan and ivory squares of thick sheep's wool. The shelves along the wall held only a small stack of books, a cassette player, and a pile of cassettes.

"Have a seat, please. I'll be right back."

He returned moments later, a glass of white zin for me, a Scotch on the rocks for himself.

"Ren, not you, the pink stuff?" I said, taking the wine.

"For you," he said, looking sheepish again. "In case you ever stopped by."

"Oh," I said. So he'd always known, even when I had not.

"And here you are."

"And here I am."

He perched on the broad arm of my chair and lifted his glass to mine.

"Cheers." Our glasses clinked. We sipped. The notes of a piano sounded softly from the speakers, and we sat quietly awkward.

"I'm so glad you came by," he said. "Did I say that already?" We both laughed.

He set his glass down and took my hand. "Come here, I want to show you something." He led me to the window. It was dark now. The moon lit the water sloshing against the docks. He stood behind me, at first giving me space, then moving in close so that his legs pressed against mine, his hands cupped my shoulders. I stood barely breathing. He pressed his lips to my cheek. I let my head rest against the crook of his neck. We watched the snow fall.

Then, he turned me to face him, and we kissed and kept on kissing the way two people will when they have waited so long and now are done waiting.

I don't know how long we stood there. Sometimes we would stop and stand, pressed together, thinking about the impossibility of what we were doing. And then we'd kiss again.

It felt like the first time I'd ever been kissed. It felt like a first crush. It felt like falling in love. It was the best feeling in the world, and it was its own hell. I pulled away.

"What is it?" Ren asked.

I shook my head. "Nothing," I breathed in, breathed out, and crossed the room to my glass of wine. "I have to go, Ren."

"No."

"I do."

"Why, Pete? Just tell me why?"

"I'm sorry. It's getting late. I promised Denny I wouldn't go running around. And I don't want the fire to go out and the cabin to get too cold."

He sighed and ran his hand over the top of his head, then looked at me, resigned, disappointed.

"Well then, if you must, I suppose you must," he said, composed and cool now. "Run on home and build your fire, make sure your pipes don't freeze."

Maybe I imagined it, but in those words I heard something that sounded very much like the superiority of my best friend's grandmother telling this eleven-year-old that she would not be returning to the country club swimming pool because it was for members only. Maybe I just needed an excuse to push him away.

"You're an ass, Ren," I said, meeting his eyes.

"And why is that, Pete? Why am I the ass?"

"You think it's so amusing that I live in a cabin in the woods. You think . . ."

"No," he cut me off. "That's not true. You don't know what I think."

"I know exactly."

"I think it's great that you are so self-sufficient. I've never known anyone who lived in a cabin, never knew a woman who chopped her own wood and built . . ."

"I don't chop my own wood," I said, which I knew sounded ridiculous. "It's only kindling."

"Oh, I beg your pardon, kindling."

"But I'll tell you one thing. I may live in a little cabin, but at least I can build my own damned fire and at least I am not stupid enough to get myself lost in the fucking woods."

I grabbed my things and slammed out the front door. The last was a low blow and I knew it. Maybe deep down, I knew the truth of that walk in the woods, or maybe I was already angry with him for what I sensed, but did not understand.

I saw the cop car about a quarter mile down our gravel road. And then a second one and a tow truck.

I pulled over to the side of the road. One of the officers shined a flashlight in my direction, his other hand rested on his gun. Instinctively, I held up my hands. He drew closer. He wasn't one I knew.

"Do you have business here?" he asked.

"I live here. About two miles up the road."

He frowned. Now the other deputy drew close. This one I knew.

"Oh hey, Pete. What are you doing out here?"

"I live out here," I said.

"Really?"

"Really."

"You recognize that car?" he asked, motioning to a dark older model Riviera the tow truck was just winching to."

I looked it over and for a second I felt a vague nag of recognition. Somewhere. When? And then it was gone.

"I guess I've seen it around town," I said. "I'm not sure."

"You see anything unusual out this way lately?"

"No, not that I can think of. What's going on?"

He shook his head. "You'll have to get that from the chief in the morning."

"Is it stolen?" I asked.

"Possibly."

"Was there anyone in it?"

He looked at me, puzzled.

"I was just thinking of the burned car they found."

"Oh. No, nothing like that."

"So, anything I should be worried about?"

"Probably not. You alone out here?"

I nodded.

"Really?"

"My husband's on the slope."

"Well, just keep your doors locked. You'll be fine."

Somehow that didn't sound as reassuring as I'd have liked. Five minutes later, I pulled up to the cabin. The Suburban headlights swept across the driveway and right off, I saw the tracks. Someone had been here. But who? It couldn't have been Ren unless he came across the lake, and I knew he wouldn't do that. Maybe it was just someone who had gotten lost or maybe it was the cops themselves driving around looking for clues into the mystery car. It was nothing. That's what I told myself.

That night I did lock both doors and for the first time wished I'd pushed Nate to put in the dead bolt he'd bought but never installed.

I hadn't been asleep long before I awoke to the sense that I had heard voices. I stayed perfectly still, barely daring to breathe, listening. But it was quiet. Maybe I'd been dreaming. Still my heart pounded, unwilling to accept such easy comfort. The numbers on the alarm clock glowed 11:01. I sat up, pulled on my sweats and tee, then lowered myself down the ladder. The porch light cast a halo over the falling snow. The world outside was quiet.

See. Nothing there. It was only a dream. I walked to the door. And that's when I saw it—or didn't. The driveway was empty. The Suburban gone. I looked two, three more times, as if somehow it would appear. I walked to the slider and peeked behind the curtain. Still nothing. How could it just be gone? I reached under the counter into the mixing bowl where I kept the .38. There was nothing there. The .38. Where the hell was the .38? I looked around the kitchen, the living room.

And then I panicked. It was foolish, I knew. The doors were locked. I had the shotgun, and yet I could not, would not, spend one more minute in that cabin alone.

I pulled on the layers of clothing, grabbed the shotgun, and hurried outside. I ripped the cover from the Cat, braced my foot on the running board, grabbed the starter with both hands, and pulled.

From across the woods came a loud bang, and I jumped at the sound echoing across the night. Gunshot? I waited and listened. Then I grabbed the pull start again and yanked until the Cat sputtered and turned over. I revved the engine, and, one hand nursing the throttle, wrapped the scarf around my face and ears and pulled on my mittens. I strapped the shotgun down along the seat and took off down the road toward the highway. But it had been plowed and sparks flew beneath me as the track fought the gravel. I turned back to the woods, picking a course between the trees. But instead of gliding across the top, the Cat struggled against the wet snow, threatening to bog down. I nudged the throttle and stood, which made it easier to maneuver but harder to dodge branches. My eyes burned, my cheeks stung. I rode out from the canopy of trees into a clearing and realized I had no idea where I was or what direction I was traveling or even where home was.

I took off across the meadow, crouched low, ducking the wind that bit at my face. I climbed a hill and rode back down, settling on a course along the bottom of a hillside where the snow was hard packed and stable. I tore around a curve, and in a whir I was yanked from the snowmobile and on the ground. Panicked, I scrambled to my feet, thinking I had to run, get away, then nearly fell back over, dizzy from the fall. I steadied myself. No one was there. But what? I turned to the snowmobile, still running, the headlight shining on an outcrop of snow that I guessed had grabbed me when I'd ridden too close. I climbed back on. There was no sign of any lights ahead. No sign of anything I could use to gauge my whereabouts. If I traveled deeper into the woods, sooner or later I'd get hung up in one of the barbed-wired fences hidden in the snow, or drop into a stream, or fall into one of the traps set for wild game. My teeth chattered. My legs burned with the cold, and I knew from all the lectures Nate had given me about hypothermia that soon they would turn numb.

I squeezed the throttle and moved slowly over the snow, then cruised through a stand of trees, across an old homestead, and up another hill. At the top I saw the vague glow of lights in the distance and rode toward them. Minutes later, I glided down a slope onto the highway. The streets were empty, Wrassell, a ghost town in white. I made my way along the shoulder until I came to the narrow lane that led to the faded red two-story. By the time I unfolded my frozen limbs from the snowmobile and crossed the deck to the front porch, he was at the door.

"Pete, you . . . my god, you're frozen . . ."

EIGHT

When I picked up the newsroom phone Saturday morning and heard Nate on the other end, I knew there could only be one reason he was calling: he knew.

"Pete, you're there," he said, sounding relieved. "Is everything OK? One of the guys at the hangar said he heard something on the scanner about the cops being called out to the cabin."

Talk about small towns.

"What's going on, Pete?"

I told him what had happened, all the way until I got to the part about getting to town. The lie that I'd spent the night curled up on the bean bag chair at the station rolled off my tongue so smoothly I realized I could almost reinvent the truth to where one day I'd believe it myself. Except I would always know. Sitting in the library wrapped in his robe, sipping Grand Marnier, falling asleep to the sound of his voice.

"I knew a woman lovely in her bones"

There was no way to tell only part of the truth about Ren. So I wouldn't tell any of it.

But just then Nate wasn't interested in where I'd spent the night.

"What did the cops say?" he asked.

"Not much. An officer came out to the cabin this morning, but he couldn't really see anything. We got more snow last night so there weren't any tracks."

"I can't believe you went out like that. What were you thinking?"

"I know. I wasn't thinking. I panicked."

"You're keeping the guns loaded, right?"

I took a deep breath. "Well, that's the other thing. I can't find the .38."

"What the hell, Pete? What do you mean you can't find the .38? Where could it have gone?"

I told him about the moose. "I thought I laid it on the breakfast bar, but I wasn't really paying attention. I was too wound up about that damned moose."

"Pete, the moose aren't going to hurt you, just . . ."

"I probably just laid it somewhere it doesn't belong. It'll turn up, I'm sure."

"What about the Scout?"

"Dan, the mechanic, just left. Some wire or something stupid came loose. It was simple. But I can tell you, I'm sick of not having a car I can count on."

"Pete, do you want me to come home?"

"You mean for a visit?"

"No, for good."

"No," I said. And then, hearing myself, more softly this time, "No, really, it's OK. We started this. Let's see it through."

I looked up from the desk and saw Ren watching me from the studio. I turned away.

"You're sure?" Nate asked. "Because I can, you know. We've got plenty in the bank, and I need to get the boat ready for fishing season anyway. I don't like this, Pete."

"I'm fine, Nate. Really." I looked up and saw Denny top the stairs. "Listen, I gotta go. Denny just got here. I'll talk to you later. Love you."

Denny was sitting at his desk, waiting for me. He looked tired. Angry, too, but in a resigned kind of way.

Over the office speakers, Connie Francis sang, *"Who's sorry now?"* I knew I'd look back one day and laugh at the irony of that one, but just then it was hard to imagine I'd ever laugh about anything.

"You didn't even lock it, did you?"

I shook my head. "No, I didn't," I said, swallowing. I wasn't about to tell him that not only had I not locked it, I'd left the keys hanging right there in the ignition. I thought that probably he was going to fire me. And I guessed I deserved it. But this was Wrassell. No one locked anything.

He lit a cigarette and threw the pack on the desk.

The phone rang.

He looked at it, annoyed at the interruption, then grabbed it from the hook.

"KWLD." And then, warmer, "Oh, morning Mona, what can I do for you?"

He listened to the voice on the other end of the phone, his expression growing worried. "But . . . well, when did you last see her? Are you sure . . . I mean. That doesn't make any sense. I'll be right there."

He hung up.

"Di never picked up Billy from the sitter last night," he said.

And in that instant, the case of the stolen Suburban became the mystery of the missing persons, one we wouldn't fully solve for months.

Chief Romer stood against the office wall while Denny paced and told him what we knew.

Di had dropped Billy with the sitter Friday evening, and said she'd be back later, then never showed. The sitter thought maybe she'd misunderstood because Billy sometimes spent the night. But Di hadn't left pajamas or even extra diapers. When morning came and still no Di, that's when the sitter got worried. Denny had run home to check the house, but there was no sign of her. She hadn't even slept in the bed.

Chief Romer asked the logical questions in his usual unflappable way, while Denny grew more annoyed by the second. It wasn't long before Denny had enough of Romer's calm.

"Listen, I'm telling you, something's happened to my wife. There's no way she would have gone off and left our son behind, damn it."

He was right. That just wasn't Di.

"There's no need to shout," Chief Romer said, patting the air with the palms of his hands. "I hear you. But nine times out of ten, these things turn out to be just a matter of miscommunication."

Denny shook his head.

"What about this missing Suburban?" Chief Romer asked. "Could she have taken it?"

"She didn't even know Pete had it," Denny said. "I never got a chance to tell her. Pete says your guys were out that way snooping around right before the Suburban disappeared. What the hell is going on? There is more to this than you're telling me."

"As you know we are in the middle of two homicide investigations . . ."

"Two?" Denny said, frowning.

Now it was my turn to be puzzled. What the hell? So, Jillian Berry wasn't one of Robert Hansen's?

"I'm sorry, I can't talk about open investigations," he said, as though reading my mind. "What I can tell you is yes, we are investigating a vehicle abandoned out that way, but there's absolutely no reason to think it has anything to do with your wife."

Denny studied the chief, scowling. I tried to make sense of what the chief had just said. What wasn't he saying?

"How do we know that whoever took the Suburban doesn't have Di, too?" Denny asked.

"I'm not following you," Chief Romer said.

"The home address and everything was in the glove box. I run a radio station. Maybe they think there's money . . ."

"I'll tell you what," the chief said, "let's go by your house and see if there's anything there. Maybe something came up and she . . ." he shrugged. "Who knows?"

Denny turned to me. "I want you to get something on the wire. Tell them, there's a woman missing, and about the Suburban, and make sure you remind them about the murders."

I watched the two walk to the chief's cruiser while I waited for the AN to answer. When the editor finally picked up, he had that hurried tone that said whatever I was calling about, I'd better be quick.

"Listen, Pete, we've got a big story breaking. What's up?"

I blurted out the story. He didn't say anything, but I could hear him shuffling paper and snippets of conversation in the background, and I wondered if he'd heard anything I'd said. He came back on the line.

I started to tell him again.

"Yeah, yeah, I heard. I'll think we'll have to take a pass on it for now, Pete. Give it a couple of days, and if no one's heard from her by then, give us a call back. Not promising anything, but we'll see. Gotta go."

Not long after, the wire clicked to life and I read the breaking story he'd referred to. An avalanche had swept the pass, taking a plow truck driver and possibly others with it. The driver had been rescued. The search was continuing.

When the next song finished, I went on the air with a special news update. Five minutes later, Skye showed up in the doorway, looking as white as the fresh snow.

"I just caught the tail end of your news," she said, breathless. "Where was the slide?"

"On the pass. Why?"

And then, tears streaming down her cheeks, she told me. The night before, Skye had gone by the station to drop off some chicken for Cork. She ran into Di a second time. Di told her she'd taken a taxi out to the cabin earlier, but I wasn't home, and asked her to give her a ride to see if I'd gotten home yet.

"Last time I saw her she was climbing into the Suburban," Skye said, sniffling.

"But why would you think . . ."

"Wait, Pete, there's something else."

"What?"

"She wasn't alone."

At the inn, I paced the creaky old wood floor, listening to the cold slop, slop, slop of the bay waters outside, replaying the story in my head. Calling up moments. The sock hop. Valentine's. The brown suede suit. Jeremy and Di. Lovers. How had we not known?

Skye didn't know where they were headed, hadn't had the nerve to ask. They could have gone anywhere. But I kept hearing Jeremy: *"So, Pete, the pass is open now, huh?"*

Still, even if they had been headed that way, it didn't mean they were there when the slide hit.

"Hey," Ren called softly, breaking my reverie. He held a snifter of Grand Marnier. I crossed the room, let him pull me to his side, closed my eyes as he kissed my forehead. We lowered ourselves to the rug, rested our backs against the leather chair. I bent my head close to the glass and breathed in its bitter citrusy scent. Until the night before I had never heard of the drink, but instantly I loved the word, loved the foreignness of it, loved watching the blue flame dance over its amber pool when Ren touched his lighter to it.

We had the radio on low, and now Mitch broke into the song, ending it in the middle."

"Listeners, we have an update on the avalanche just in from the AN. Search-and-rescue teams have found a second vehicle and confirmed there are at least two fatalities."

"Oh no." I covered my mouth and listened.

Mitch continued. "Police have not released identities, but the AN is reporting that an anonymous source has identified the vehicle as a newer model Ford Taurus stolen from a parking lot in recent days. Police have called off the search, and say they do not believe there are any other victims. Now, the Temptations."

"It's not them," I said. I let out a breath and sank my head back against the chair. It wasn't them. The relief was fleeting, replaced by the new worry that we still had no idea where they were, if they were OK. "Where could they have gone, Ren? It just doesn't make any sense."

Ren squeezed my hand. "My guess is, Denny's going to get a call any time now that they found the truck at the airport and sooner or later probably a call from Di from someplace like sunny Hawaii."

"But Billy. I would have never believed she'd leave him," I said.

"I know. That puzzles me, too."

"Except, really when you think about it, she pretty much abandoned her other two. And running away with a two-year-old isn't exactly a romantic escape. God, poor Denny. I wonder if he knew."

"Oh, I think most spouses do. Whether or not they want to admit it to themselves is a different story."

"That's why you and your wife split up, isn't it?"

"I was hoping you'd never ask that."

"But it is, isn't it?"

He took a sip of his drink, then studied it, rattling the ice. "You get over it. Denny will, too."

"And here we are," I said.

"Don't," he said.

He squeezed my hand and turned to me. He had a way of looking at me with such tenderness, I couldn't help but smile. Then, he grew serious. "There's something I need to tell you," he said. "I owe you an apology."

"For what?"

"Yesterday, I don't know what I was thinking…" He paused and I felt his body tense. "Did you hear that?" he said, whispering now.

"What?" I whispered back. "Did I hear what?

Before he could answer, there was a knock on the door. I turned to him. He held a finger up to his lips.

"Who is it?" I asked.

He shook his head.

There was another rap, sharper this time.

"Ren?" A woman's voice called. "Ren, are you there?" She knocked again. He looked down at his hands folded in his lap. "Ren? Ren, are you in there? Come on, Ren, it's me, open up."

He tipped his head back against the leather chair and closed his eyes, then opened them again. "How cruel of me," he whispered.

"Answer it," I urged, whispering. "Why don't you answer it?"

But he just sat silently holding my hand all the harder.

"Ren," she called, knocking hard now, over and over. We waited, barely breathing. The pounding stopped. I could sense her listening. Then finally, we heard her footsteps crunch across the deck, a car door open and close, and the car move slowly away, its sound growing faint until she was gone.

"How cruel," he said again.

"Your girlfriend?" I asked.

"No. Not at all. Just Belinda. I promised I would go with her to a movie."

"Well then, why didn't you go?"

"Because I'm here with you."

"But Ren."

"But nothing."

He turned to me, those blue eyes so tender, so serious, and in that moment every single thing in the world mattered less than the fact of him, of us, of the reality that we did not have forever, but only now.

Naked, he was so thin, and yet there was a perfect proportion to his body and a sureness that was not arrogance, but knowing. He moved along my body with an awareness of every sensation he created, drawing it out, until my skin hummed. When it was time, he held himself away, so that I had to reach for him. And then as I arched my back, toes curling, he took the ride home, too.

When it was over, and we lay side by side, each with our cigarette and contentedness, I knew that in the morning, or at least some morning, I would feel the guilt, but that for the rest of my life, right there next to that guilt, would be the satisfaction of knowing the feel of his skin against mine, of hearing him say my name. It would be something. Something to keep in some corner, to take out and relive on some day far away when I could afford such a luxury. It would have to be enough.

We left his place while the world slept oblivious and dreaming, still under a night black sky. The highway was empty, shops dark. The clock on the bank sign read 4:07. I wanted to go home to my own bed. It was one thing to make love to him, but staying there, facing the new day next to him seemed to compound the wrong. I guess there are some things better faced in the dark.

I reached for the volume on the radio, and heard the sound every jock dreads, dead air.

"Do you hear that?" I asked.

"Sounds like the mic's open."

"But how can that be? We sign off now at midnight. No one's supposed to be there until five."

"Maybe the engineer came by to work on something and forgot?"

We pulled into the parking lot. The station was dark save for the glow of a table lamp in the control room. The Scout was sitting where it had been since Friday. Next to it was the station wagon Di was to have left at the shop.

"How odd," Ren said.

"Denny must have picked it up," I said.

I opened the car door and climbed out.

"Pete, wait. What are you doing," he said, following me.

"I'm going to see what's going on."

"You think that's a good idea?"

"Well, we can't just let the microphone sit open like that. Anyone listening can hear it. Denny'll have a fit."

"We should wait and call the police and let them check it out."

"Right, and say what? Send help, we don't hear anything?"

"Well, we . . . never mind," he said, looking embarrassed.

I pulled open the door, and turned to him. "It should have been locked."

"I don't like this, Pete." He looked nervous, and I couldn't help but note that had it been Nate, he would have already been charging up the stairs. He would have known exactly what to do.

"Well, wait here then," I said.

"You're tough," he sighed, stepping in front of me. "Let's get this over with."

We paused, listening, eyes adjusting to the dark, broken only by the glow of the Exit sign at the top. It occurred to me if anyone was up there they would wonder about the two of us together in those wee hours, and they would know. And then I brushed the thought away because there was nothing to be done about it anyway.

"Denny?" Ren called.

Nothing.

"Di?" I tried.

We looked at each other. "Doesn't sound like there's anyone up there," I said.

He started up the stairs. I followed. At the top, he flipped the light switch. The room was empty. But the sign over the control room glowed red, warning of an open microphone.

Ren started toward the room and I followed. The door was open just a crack. Ren hesitated, and then pushed it open.

"Oh Jesus," he said.

Inside, Denny was sprawled on the floor beneath the control panel, the mic dangling above him. Next to him was an empty fifth of Scotch. His face was white, his body deathly still.

"Call 911," Ren yelled.

The medics took Denny away. Ren followed. I stayed at the station to answer questions from the police and find someone to do the morning shift. It wasn't long before the phones began to ring, people wanting to know what was going on, was Denny OK? It got to the point where I just let it ring. Then, the news line flashed. I picked up.

"Pete, Brady here. What the hell is going on over there?"

"Why? What did you hear?"

"Everything," she said. "What a mess, and to think poor Uncle Chris was actually talking about buying the place. Talk about a scandal. The whole bay is talking about it, Pete. Even all the way down here."

"What are they saying?" I asked.

"Plenty. About Di and the a.m. jock. About the scene she made at the jewelry store when she tried to return her diamond for cash and couldn't because it was a trade."

"Seriously?"

"You didn't know?"

"No."

"I guess you're going to tell me you didn't know your GM was on the air drunk in the middle of the night, huh?"

"Oh, come on. That's not true."

"Pretty much incoherent."

"Who told you that?'

"Who? Everybody. Our sound engineer is an insomniac. He heard him."

"Oh my God," I said.

"Yeah, see what I mean. It's ridiculous."

"You're not going to do anything on this, are you, Kate? I mean, it's not news."

"Are you kidding me? Not news? The general manager of a radio station goes on the air drunk, downs an entire fifth of alcohol, nearly killing himself, and it's not news. Jesus, pally, it's a fucking scandal you could probably sell to the *National Enquirer*." She paused. And then, "But no, Pete, I'm not going to do anything. Believe it or not, my heart is not a complete black hole."

Later that morning, the AN named the two victims in the avalanche: Roberta Gooding and Randy Wells. I didn't recognize either one.

The hospital released Denny that same day. Ren thought it was a mistake. I wanted to believe it meant he wasn't so bad off as we feared.

"He told them it was an accident," Ren said. "But how the hell do you accidentally down an entire fifth of Scotch?"

"Well, they wouldn't have released him if he wasn't OK, would have they?"

"I think they should have kept him, at least overnight. It seems pretty obvious to me that he tried to drink himself to death."

"Oh shit, Ren. This is Denny we're talking about. If he'd wanted to kill himself, he would have. He's not one of your Sylvia Plath types, trust me."

"Really?" he said. "Sylvia Plath type. I wonder, Pete, what type is that exactly?"

Neither of us said anything for a moment. And then he kind of sighed and said he guessed he'd better be on his way, and he did it in such a quiet, disappointed way, I thought that was probably the end of us, and I knew it was just as well, but I missed him the second he disappeared out that door.

Annie's was nearly deserted, save for a handful of regulars and Skye, who was at the end of the bar, bent over a notepad.

"Hey Skye. Mind?"

She shook her head no and gathered her things to make room for me at the stool next to her. "I'm writing Kyle a letter," she said. "I figured he'd want to know."

I felt a pang. I hadn't finished my letter. Hadn't even given it—
or him for that matter—a thought. The world had changed just as
I feared it would. There would be no going back.

"Hey, did you hear about the couple killed in the avalanche?"
Skye asked, tossing her long hair over her shoulder.

"What about them?"

"She was a dancer at the Cherry Cabaret. I used to deliver to
their apartment. Only she went by Robyn."

"Robyn? Robyn with the long hair and really pretty eyes?"

"Yeah."

"That was her?

Skye nodded.

"I knew her," I said. "I knew her from a few years back when she
went by Bobbie. That was her? She died?"

"And her boyfriend."

"That's horrible," I said.

"It is. But if you want to be honest about it, she wasn't exactly
the nicest woman in the world. He was OK. He always tipped decent—at least when she wasn't around. They were in a stolen car,
you know that?"

"Yeah, I heard that. She stole a pair of Danskins from me once."

Skye knitted her eyebrows. "Danskins? Where in the world
were you wearing Danskins and what were you doing hanging with
her?"

"Never mind. Nothing good. But wow, what a terrible way to go.
I think you suffocate. Slowly."

"I know. At least it wasn't Di."

Annie came out from the back room. "You guys hear anything?"

We shook our heads. "You?" I asked.

She sighed. "No. I'm surprised. I really am."

"Surely, she'll come back for the wedding," Skye said. "Or at
least send something."

"I would think so," Annie said. "I can't imagine she would just disappear without so much as a, 'See you around.' I just don't know what to think."

The tavern door swooped open behind us. We turned.

Ren looked grim.

"What happened, Ren?" I asked. But I guess I already knew.

NINE

Denny's dream on Melody Lane ended with a nervous breakdown, a straitjacket, and a guest room in a psych ward somewhere in the Midwest near his mother.

I never even got to say good-bye.

I called George and explained the best I could. He listened quietly, then sighed. "Can't say I'm surprised. About the wife, maybe. But not Denny. I should have known better. I'm going to have to do some thinking. I'll get back to you."

And that was how we left it. Just hanging there. We knew it was only a matter of time. We kept on anyway, playing spots that had long run out, trading air time for chicken hearts and doing live plugs for whatever else we needed—a favor from the engineer, a new headset from the electronic shop. Until someone said "Stop," we would just go on. It wasn't like there was anywhere else to go.

When we were not at the station, Ren and I inhabited our own little world at the inn, falling quickly into a routine as if we'd been doing it forever. Always, we sat in the library, side by side, backs against that wide red chair. We listened to music: George Winston, Miles Davis, Burt Bacharach, the soundtrack from *Breakfast at Tiffany's*, Ren's favorite. He was relic, but I didn't care. He was my relic.

And we talked. We talked about books—Had I read *The Alexandria Quartet*? About poetry. Roethke and Eliot were his favorites. He loved "The Waste Land," and could go on and on from memory.

> *April is the cruellest month, breeding*
> *Lilacs out of the dead land, mixing*
> *Memory and desire, stirring*
> *Dull roots with spring rain.*

We talked about the places he'd been, and the places I wanted to go. Sometimes, we just sat quietly, content in each other's company. Too late, I would find I knew almost nothing about Ren.

I knew that he been named a Fulbright scholar to Oxford, and that only days after had received his draft notice. I knew that he came from money. I knew that he adored his Italian mother who dressed in high heels and gloves and loved the opera and who died of breast cancer no one knew she had while he was in Vietnam. I knew that he loved me and that he thought I was smart and fearless. Fearless. Maybe once, in my own way I was, but after him, I would never be quite so again.

That I didn't know enough about him never even occurred to me because I had no idea it was all there would be. But I should have. He tried to tell me. I just wasn't listening.

It was an April evening, the clouds leaking relentless rain. By then the potholes had filled with muddy runoff, gutters overflowed in dirty slush.

"Ren, breakup. It's here."

"So it is."

"And you were the one who wasn't going to stick around."

"I wasn't."

"I'm glad you did."

"Me, too."

"So OK, why did you come here? Honestly."

"I told you, I wanted to see Alaska. Maybe I knew I was supposed to meet you."

"Fate, huh?" I said, trying for a lightness I didn't feel.

"Sure seems that way to me," he said.

"You could still change your mind, you know. Stick around. Fix this place up like Denny wanted you to." And then, with a wave of wistfulness I hadn't expected, "I love it here," I said, and felt the words catch in my throat.

"I know," he said. "And when you're here, I love it too." He reached for my hand. "But you won't always be here, will you?"

"No. I'm sorry."

"I know," he said, kissing my temple.

Oh, the deals I might have struck if only we could have had that moment forever, if only I could have figured out a way to have it all.

On the stereo, someone sounded the low, hopeful notes of "Blue Velvet" on a horn. Ren stood, and I let him pull me to my feet, and we danced, small swaying steps by the window, neither of us saying anything now. Outside, rain rippled the dark bay waters, and tapped against the paned glass, and far beyond, the light of a fishing boat flickered as it moved toward home. Soon it would be summer. The fish would be jumping. The tourists would come with their campers and questions and wide-eyed ignorance. The days would last forever and the nights not nearly long enough. The foil would go up on apartment windows to block the light, the bug dope would multiply then just as quickly disappear from the store shelves. Someone would win the fishing derby. Jack and Annie would get married. Nate would come home. And all of this would be so much history. Life would go on.

"I've never had a love affair with life, Pete." He said it quietly, mouth close to my ear, and I had to replay the words in my head to make sure I'd heard.

I pulled back so I could see his face. "What do you mean?"

He shrugged.

"No, Ren. Tell me."

He put his mouth against my hair and breathed, "There was a time, back in college when I was ready, when I tried to . . . Well, you know, me and Sylvia Plath."

"Ren, that's not funny."

"It's OK."

"But that was then, in the past, right?"

He was quiet.

"You'd never do anything like that now. Right?" I insisted.

He nodded. "Right."

And I believed him. Because I had to.

We figured George would shutter the place. Instead, he sent Harold, his accountant brother. Harold was a ruddy-haired, clean-shaven man, given to short-sleeved button-down shirts, polyester slacks, and sensible shoes. He looked like a man without a musical note in his body.

We tried to resist Harold. It seemed the loyal thing to do, but if we were cool and distant, he didn't seem to notice, and we soon came around to the realization that he wasn't going anywhere. He didn't know much about radio, but he had these wild notions about computers and how soon everything in the station would by operated by them. We just listened and nodded along and secretly wondered if he was a little nuts. But we soon figured out that whatever else he may or may not have known, he understood the business world, and before long we began to feel like a real radio station again. We picked up new advertisers, and Harold began looking to build up our staff, and not just DJs, but real sales people, too.

One day Harold gathered us in the break room to introduce a new jock. His name was Terry. He was tall and skinny with a thick wave of black hair, like the dot on an exclamation mark.

Terry was from Colorado and had already found himself an apartment and was ready to go, Harold said. "So I want to take this moment to both welcome Terry and to say so long to Ren, who tells me he is off on a new adventure, and to whom I owe a huge debt of gratitude . . ."

It was the first I'd heard of it, and it caught me like a slap. Ren tried to get my attention, but I ignored him. When Harold finished, I hurried back to the newsroom, closed the door, and huddled over the typewriter.

There was a tap on the door, and then it opened a crack. I kept typing, pounding out the words of a fictional weather report. Ren leaned inside, holding a white Wings 'N Things bag out in front him. "Piece of my heart?"

"Sorry, I have to get the eleven o'clock news together," I said, still banging on those keys. He waited, and I knew he was hurt to be so easily dismissed.

"Close the door, please," I said.

He took a step in closer. "Pete? Talk to me."

"I told you. I'm busy."

"Pete, I didn't even know myself until this morning. But you've seen all the people he's hiring. There's really no reason for me to be here. I meant to tell you, honestly, this afternoon as soon as you got off and we had some time together. And then Harold beat me to it."

"It's fine," I said. "Really, I'll talk to you later. I've got a couple of stories I need to get finished now." But there were no stories, only an emptiness in the pit of my stomach and a sob waiting to erupt.

"Let me take you out tonight," he said.

"Go, Ren. I have to be on the air in ten minutes. Don't do this to me."

"Then say yes. A real date."

He picked me up at the cabin in the Mercedes. I wore a skirt, heels, and a strand of pearls I'd gotten for signing up for a credit card.

"You look lovely, Patrice. I don't believe I've ever seen you in a skirt."

"Thanks," I said, feeling suddenly shy and uncertain.

"And pearls."

"They're not real," I said.

Ren smiled that smile of tender amusement. "Really?" he said and kissed me.

We had reservations at the Glacier House. It was the place where people who knew which fork to use when went, people like Kate Brady, whose pearls were surely real. There was a time I wouldn't have cared.

We pulled into a mostly empty parking lot. I waited for him to come around and open my door, and took his arm, let him hold the door.

Inside, the Glacier House was dark. White tablecloths, red carpet, black chairs, black napkins. Silver. Candles. A pianist. Just like I thought it would be.

The maître d' said it would be just a moment, and Ren led me to a dark leather bench against the wall. I crossed my feet at my ankles and tucked them beneath the bench, folded my hands in my lap. From the opposite side of the wall, a woman's mannered chortles cut the silence, joined by a second, and then, the quieter chuckles from the men. I imagined them, fixed blonde bobs and pearls, real pearls. They were the Buffys and Skips of the bay, the people who showed up in the society photos that ran during the holidays when the hospital hosted its annual fund-raiser. Ren caught my eye and then seeing my expression leaned forward and kissed my forehead and smiled a smile that said, *We'll have a good time. Really.*

"Let's go," I said.

"What . . . are you OK?"

"Let's just get out of here," I said with a desperation I hadn't even realized I was feeling.

"Sure." We stood just as the maître d' approached. Ren met him, murmured something, and slipped him a bill.

Outside, it was pouring. "You wait here, I'll get the car," he said over the percussion of the downpour. "It's OK. I can run." He looked at me, took my hand, and we ran through the rain to the Mercedes, dropping into our seats breathless, wet, and laughing.

Finally, laughing.

We told the woman at the front desk we were bound for Paris, by way of Seattle, squeezing hands as we indulged in our game of make believe.

Except for one man watching TV, the club room was empty. We took the same spot in the corner by the gas fireplace. Ren fetched us two flutes of champagne, a plate of strawberries and cheese. "Cheers," he said.

I raised my glass, but what was there to cheer? This was the beginning of our good-bye, the last time we would embark on our fantasy travel.

"Hey," Ren said, reaching across the table for my hand. "Did you know there's a place where when it freezes, you can walk to Russia?"

"Ass," I said.

"But it made you smile."

"You probably shouldn't tell people that. I don't even know if it's true."

"All the more reason . . ."

"Where will you go?" I asked in a voice that had turned all wobbly, as if there was a bubble in my throat the words had to roll over. "You've never said." He put his finger to my lips. "Ssshhh."

We watched a jet taxi down the runway, water spraying from the black tires. It stopped, gave a shudder, and aimed for the sky.

"I won't see you again then, will I?"

"I don't know. Will you?" He took a swallow of champagne and squeezed my hand harder, but I noticed he was avoiding my eyes. "Actually, no," he said. "Probably not."

"Probably not," I repeated. My lip started to curl in that embarrassing way it did when I was about to cry.

A tear spilled over and streaked down my cheek. "Great, now my mascara will run," I said.

He pressed the back of his hand against my cheek, blotting it dry.

"I'll miss you, too," he said.

I tipped the champagne flute to my lips, tilted my head back, and swallowed the half glass that remained.

"Here, I'll get you another."

When he returned, he set the glass in front of me, leaned across the table, and took my hand.

"Come away with me. Away from the bay. For a weekend. Where no one knows us and we can just be us."

"I can't leave."

"Of course, you can. Why not?"

"But . . . where would we go?"

"Wherever you want. The bay. The real bay. San Francisco."

"San Francisco. I've never been."

"We'll get a suite. Something with a fireplace and hot tub looking over the water."

"When?" I said.

"This weekend."

"You can get tickets that soon?"

"Of course. Ask Harold for some time off. We'll catch a flight Friday morning."

TEN

The trick to loving two men, I was learning, was to pretend that one did not exist. Except, I never said, not even to myself, that I loved Ren, only that I liked him so much. It was not the wild, crazy passion I had felt for Nate, but a dearness in my heart, a sense of such genuine affection, that for years after it could make me want to cry just remembering it.

"Hey, I hear you're going to San Francisco," Terry said, standing in the doorway, fingers hooked over the top so he could stretch. "Lucky girl. One of my favorite cities in the world. Ever been?"

"First time."

"Well, you know what they say," he said, singing a line, "*If you're going to San Francisco,*" he paused and pointed to my phone. "I'll catch up with you later."

I slipped on the headset, flipped the switch to phone.

"KWLD newsroom," I said.

"Hey, Babe . . ."

"Nate," I said, my heart pounding like one caught in the act.

Two days later, Nate strode across the asphalt, backpack over his shoulder, faded jeans, work boots, that cocky smile that said *Hey, world, here I am, and here's my girl, and ain't life grand.* People turned to look at him, he was that good looking—dark eyes, dimpled chin, dark hair long now, and caught at the nape of his neck in a rubber band—but Nate didn't notice.

He stepped inside. I opened my mouth to say his name, but nothing came. He dropped his bag and wrapped his arms around me, then stepped back. "You're just as perfect as I remembered."

I didn't know if I was going to laugh or cry. I knew I was supposed to be excited, but mostly I just felt overwhelmed. Nate had faded in my memory like an old Polaroid. Now, here he was, as alive and handsome as ever. But I needed time. Just a little more time.

"That was a big sigh," Nate said.

"You're here. I can't believe you're really here. It's been so long." It was supposed to be one of those enthusiastic, I'm-so-excited kind of things, but it came out sounding forced and insincere. If Nate noticed, he did a good job of pretending otherwise.

He threw his duffle bag in the back. I started for the driver's door, then saw he was headed for the same.

"You want to drive?" he asked.

"No, go ahead," I said.

I slid in the passenger side.

He reached his hand across the seat and took mine. "It's been a long time."

"All of five months," I said.

"Whew," he said. "Almost half a year."

"It was a long time to be alone," I said.

"It was a long time to be away. But here we are. We made it."

I tried to think of something bright to say, but all I could think of was it had been long, too long. And yes, we had made it, but at what cost? And how was I going to go on?

He squeezed my hand. "God, I missed you."

We pulled into the cabin driveway.

"Wow. I almost forgot. The cabin. It looks good, Pete." Then, eyeing the woodpile, "Hey, I guess it's a good thing I came home after all. It looks like you're just about out of wood."

"After all?" I said.

He shrugged. "Oh, I didn't mean it that way. Just that you've managed pretty well on your own. I can tell."

Inside the cabin, he took a look around, then went to the slider to let himself out on the deck. He tugged on the handle.

"What's up with the door?"

"Oh, sorry, I forgot," I said, reaching down to move the piece of metal the locksmith Ren had sent had given me to lay in the track.

"After everything that happened, I guess I got a little spooked."

"I don't blame you. I should have gotten you something like that before I left. A piece of doweling works just as well. I just didn't think." He sighed, turned up his palms.

"It's OK. I survived."

He leaned in and kissed me. "I'm going to get a shower and then I'll be right out." He was halfway across the room. He stopped and turned back to me. "You can always join me, you know."

He dropped his clothing to a pile on the bathroom floor, and I must say Nate naked was a thing to behold. His stomach was flat and bumpy with muscles, split by a dark line of curls snaking up to his belly button; his shoulders wide, angling down to narrow hips. There wasn't a woman in the world who wouldn't have wanted him. What was wrong with me?

I shed my jeans and blouse and stepped into the shower beside him. He moved over to make room for me and kissed me on the nose, then went about shampooing his hair.

I soaped my calf and ran the razor from ankle to knee, though I'd just shaved that same leg not three hours earlier. Nate soaped up, handed the bar back to me. I shaved the other leg. It occurred to me for the first time that maybe he wasn't so thrilled to be back, either. Maybe he'd come to like being away. Maybe he didn't have any more of an idea of what to do than I did.

He stood beneath the water, letting it rinse the lather from his body. I stepped into the stream to rinse my legs. He took my hand and pulled me closer, and just for an instant, looked at me—Was this OK?—and then we kissed and we kept kissing until we ran out of air. We came up, and kissed some more. He cupped his hand between my legs, fingers searching beneath the curls, then found a rhythm, strumming, driving me up on tiptoe, and I had to brace my hand against the shower wall for fear my knees wouldn't hold. I wrapped my other hand around him and stroked. We kissed, teeth mashing against lips, sucking air when we could, hands moving faster, bodies demanding more, harder, now. Trembling and out of breath, we ducked from the water, gasping for air, then slumped against each other beneath the steady pour. When I had caught my breath, I stepped back, pushed the hair from my face and seeing him, wet and satisfied, caught a glimpse of what used to be.

"Welcome home," I said.

Summer and money changed everything. We bought a Ford Bronco and paid the phone company to run the line to our house. Nate put his boat on the river and right off his old customers from the summer before began filling the books.

When days, then a week, went by with no sign of Ren, I knew I needed to make peace with the fact that he was gone. And I knew I should be glad, that eventually it would make things easier. But I missed him, and I guessed I would for a long time.

I had seen him last when I had gone to the inn to tell him the news. It was our last night, and we knew that, and it seemed we couldn't find a damned thing to say. And so we had sat like two people grieving, holding hands, until there was nothing left but for me to go.

He said, "Let me see you tomorrow. Stay the night. Let me take you to dinner.

"I can't," I'd said, and I meant it because every minute I spent with him, I grew less able to leave, and I feared if I didn't just get out of there my feet might fail me completely.

He said, "*I knew a woman lovely in her bones . . .*"

And I wished just once I had something beautiful to say to him.

We said we wouldn't say good-bye. And we didn't. Not even so long. What I remember about leaving was that I could not look back, and I could not look forward. I couldn't even think, really, just move, one foot in front of the other.

This was it. The end. Except, I didn't really believe that. What I really thought was that one day he'd come back, and we would sneak off for a glass of wine and laugh about old times. And we would be friends. Just friends.

Then, one afternoon Nate and I went for groceries. I was pushing my cart, reading my list, generally lost in my own little world of price comparisons and coupon deals, and there was Ren by the coffee. I hurried past, my heart pounding, through the paper towels and tissues and cleaning supplies, the condiments and canned goods, through the frozen food, and not another sign of him. I began to relax. He was gone. And then I began to regret it and wished for just another glimpse, a chance to send him a smile—to catch his eyes and for an instant connect.

I rounded the corner of the last aisle, dairy and produce, and there he was. He saw me then, and just for the fleetest of seconds our eyes met, and I had to turn for fear my face would give something away, and Nate would see.

"I think this is everything," I said, though I would get home and find I hadn't picked up the half of it. We steered the cart to the checkout. Minutes later, as I unloaded the groceries on the black conveyor belt, I heard his voice at the register next to me, and looked up.

"Hello Patrice," he said. "How are you?"

"Fine," I said. "And you?"

"I'm well, thank you." He picked up his bag, raised his hand, good-bye. "Take care," he said, and he was gone.

"Who was that?" Nate asked.

"Nobody," I said. "Just someone who helped out at the station once in a while."

The next day, I picked up the newsroom line. "How are you?" he said in that tender way of his.

"I'm fine," I said. "Good. I mean, not really. How about you?"

"Fine. Lousy. I'm sorry, I said I wouldn't bother you."

"No. It's OK. I'm glad you did. I've been thinking about you."

"You have?"

"Of course."

"I miss you, Pete."

I didn't say anything, for fear that somehow the wrong words would tumble out, and I would be weak and agree to see him just one more time.

"Actually, I just wanted to say good-bye," he said.

"Good-bye? We weren't going to. Remember?"

"Yes, of course, that's right. Still, it seems there should be something. Don't you think?"

"How about, So long?" I said, feigning lightness, as if by pretending it could be so.

"Yes, that's better, isn't it," he said. "Or we could say 'Farewell' or '*Ciao*.' So many ways to say what we weren't going to."

"We don't have to. It doesn't have to be so final, you know."

"Au revoir, Pete."

"Where are you going?"

"I'm not sure, really."

"You could call some time," I said. "Just, you know, so I can hear how you are."

"Yeah?"

"Don't just disappear with me never knowing what became of you."

"I'll try," he said.

"Promise me."

"Think of me sometimes, will you?" And then he was gone.

I generally napped afternoons so when Nate got in, I could spend some time with him. But that day he had engine problems and got in early, just before 6:00. We were outside on the deck, talking. We were still catching up on things, remembering this, reminding each other of that. In that way, we wove our lives back together, and I had begun to feel settled again.

"You know, Annie and Jack's wedding is less than two weeks away, and we need to buy you a suit," I said.

"Can't I just wear a pair of decent jeans and my sports jacket?"

"No. I don't want you to look like some hick. This is a big wedding. People will be dressed."

He took a sip of his beer. "Babe, it's Wrassell. People don't dress here—not like that."

I thought of Ren and those perfect white Oxfords. "I don't care what other people do, Nate," I said. "I want you to look like you have some class. Like we're not country bumpkins living in the sticks."

"Country bumpkins, Patrice?" he teased.

"You know what I mean, and since when do you call me Patrice?"

"Since when does anyone?"

So he'd noticed. "It's my name. And you know that no one who knows me calls me that. You're going to need a tie, too."

A mosquito buzzed my ear, and I smacked myself in the head trying to slap it away. "Ouch, damn it," I said. Most people thought the long dark winters made Alaska unbearable, but the fact was, the snow and short days were nothing compared to the mosquitoes. The mosquitoes, jokingly referred to as the state bird, could drive a person nuts.

"Yup, typically that's what one wears with a suit," Nate said. He sighed and took a long swallow from his beer. "I suppose I have to buy new shoes, too?"

Another mosquito had settled on my arm. I flicked it away, but it had already drawn blood. "Oh fuck it," I said. "Wear what you want. Is it so terrible that I want you to look nice?"

"And not like some hick?" he said.

"I never said you look like a hick."

"Of course not."

We sat in silence, sipping our drinks, staring off at distant places. How had we gotten here?

"I never said you look like a hick," I said. "I just meant, it's a big day . . . never mind."

"It's OK," he said. "I know what you meant. I guess I never knew you cared so much what people thought."

"Well, I do," I said.

"I'll try to keep that in mind."

He let a few minutes pass, then reached across the table and took my hand. "Blondie, since when do we fight about silly things like what to wear to someone's wedding?"

I shrugged.

"What's on your mind, Pete?"

"Nothing."

"You're quieter these days. You don't bubble like you used to."

"Bubble? I never bubbled, Nate."

"Sure you did." He leaned across the table and kissed me. "I have to go to the pawn shop to look for a tool. Maybe they'll have a used suit there."

"And you would probably buy it," I said.

"I probably would. Coming along?"

"I think I'll pass," I said. "But hey, I've meaning to say, Annie asked me to go hunting for moose this fall. I guess I'll need a gun my own size. Maybe you could take a look and see what he has."

"Sure," he said. "Hunting, huh?"

"What do you think?"

"That's fine if you think that's what you want to do. But, Pete . . ."

"Hmmm?"

"Have you thought about how you'll feel about killing something?"

The next morning, the DA's secretary called to say there would be a press conference at 10:00.

I canned my ten o'clock news and hurried from the newsroom. Outside, I breathed in the air and immediately picked up the sweet smell of fire, followed seconds later by the wail of sirens. But there was no time. It would have to wait.

At the courthouse, I set up my mic and recorder on the table up front and took a seat next to the guy from the *Daily Wrassellite*. I watched the door for Kate, but at two minutes to she still hadn't come.

Bidarkee Bay Borough DA Celia St. Clair strode into the room and took the podium. She was a petite woman, with a turkey neck and the unfortunate habit of bobbing her head all the time.

"Everyone ready?" she asked.

We nodded. I felt bad for Kate because I knew how I'd feel, but I loved the idea that if it was something big, it was all mine to break.

"As you know, earlier this spring an avalanche claimed the lives of a man and a woman we identified as Roberta Gooding and Randy Wells," St. Clair began, reading from a page in front of her. "At the time it was also revealed that the two were in a stolen car. Incidentally, we had located a car registered to Mr. Wells in a rural area out by Lasso Lake just days before the avalanche. At that time, we were already investigating the pair for several crimes and were about to make our arrest.

"Today, through our investigation and the evidence seized, we can say with absolute certainty that Ms. Gooding and Mr. Wells were responsible for the deaths of Jillian Berry and Adam Kuro-sawa."

I listened as she told a tale that stretched back years before when Bobbie/Robyn/Roberta had been involved in another murder, the charges of which she escaped in part by providing air-tight alibis. One of those was Jillian Berry. "We believe Jillian Berry was murdered after she attempted to extort money in exchange for her silence. Mr. Kurosawa had a long-running relationship with Ms. Berry. We believe he suspected the truth and came to see what he could find out. All of this might have been avoided had Ms. Berry gone to the police in the first place. And surely Mr. Kurosawa would still be alive if he had also sought help from the authorities."

I wrote the story in my head as I drove like a crazy woman back to the studio. This was the story I'd been waiting months to break. And here it was, mine. But until I saw those words printing out under my name I'd have no peace.

"Big news?" Terry called as I passed the studio.

"Oh yeah."

He followed me, "Find out anything about the fire?"

"No time. I'll check on it as soon as I get this done."

I was dialing the AN when the printer started up. I rushed over, and right off saw the KBAY call letters. But how? Someone had tipped her off. Someone would always tip off the Kate Brady's of the world. I read as it printed and soon saw it had nothing to do with the press conference. It was the fire. A fatality. Then I saw the name, but even as I felt my stomach dip in recognition, I wasn't thinking Ren. I was thinking some relative, someone must have visited. I wasn't used to the whole Reynolds thing, and I'd forgotten all about the three Roman numerals at the end of his name. Reynolds Kennedy III. Then the truth, the reality of what I was reading, crept into my awareness, sweeping over me in a wave that buckled my knees and stole my breath.

In that moment, I understood the meaning of darkness.

In the days that followed, I learned to mourn Ren on my own time—the afternoon hours before Nate got in and the wee hours he laid sleeping unaware beside me. The rest of the time I operated on autopilot, thinking as little as possible. When I needed to cry, I took long aimless walks, often as not in the rain, which I grew to love for all it hid and because there was something fitting about being cold and soaked and without shelter.

Nate knew that Ren had set fire to the inn, then shot himself, and he knew that Ren had sometimes helped out at the radio station, and that he was my friend. Those moments when he looked at me in a way that suggested I was taking things awfully hard, I said something about suicide and never knowing anyone before, and that Ren had been such a nice guy. Nate said he was sorry, really sorry about it. If he knew that Ren was the guy from the grocery store—*Hello, Patrice*—he never said. And I didn't bother pointing it out.

The day after we got the news, I went to the inn on my lunch break. I don't know what I hoped to find, except I desperately wanted some sign, something to say he was still with us. Still with me. That I would never speak to him again, never hear his voice, was unfathomable.

The fire damage was minimal, I'd heard, contained mostly to the library. From outside, you couldn't tell there'd been a fire, except for the smell. One of the Wrassell cops was locking up the place.

"Which funeral home did they take him to?" I asked from the window. There were two on the bay.

He shook his head. "His family had him shipped out of state."

"But what about a funeral?"

He shrugged. "Don't ask me. I just do what they tell me to do. The chief left this morning for vacation. He can probably tell you something when he gets back. He's the one who spoke with the family."

Annie and Jack and a few of us at the station talked about having some sort of memorial, but there were hardly any of us left who really knew him, and it being a suicide seemed to somehow make it different from just any other death. In the end, we gathered at Annie's.

We told Ren stories, the light stuff. We laughed. I tried to focus on all the good memories and not think too much about the truth of why we were there. That he was dead. Gone. I was never in my entire life going to see, hear, or talk to him again. About the time everyone was on their third drink, and people started getting teary, I started thinking about all the Ren stories I would never get to tell.

About the poetry and Paris and walking to Russia . . . I left then and went home to dwell in those memories alone.

A week later, on the eve of Annie's wedding, I was sitting on the deck alone. Sleep didn't come so easily those days and naps were out of the question. I heard the tires crunching in the gravel, and stood, expecting to see Nate. Instead, I saw Chief Romer pulling into the drive. He looked like a man with a purpose, a man on official business. I walked out to the driveway. He stepped from the car just as Nate turned the corner.

"Evening, Pete," the chief said.

"Hey, Chief," I said, and right off I felt a sense of alarm. He had a way about him that suggested he'd rather not be there doing whatever he'd come to do.

He pulled the plastic stirrer from his mouth. "Pete, any idea how this Kennedy fellow would have gotten ahold of your gun?"

He gazed up at me from under the lank of black hair.

"My gun? What do you mean?"

"The .38 you reported missing?"

"My .38? No."

I tried to make sense of what the chief was saying, to somehow explain to him why he was wrong. Except, he wasn't and I knew it. I remembered Ren standing on the porch. *"Hey, by the way, you really should lock your door."* Ren with the confession he started to make in the library but never finished and I never asked about because I thought he'd meant only to tell me he had agreed to take Belinda to the movies. But what if he had told me the truth and given me back the gun? What would it have mattered? Ren had always been looking for a way, I saw that now—the walk in the woods. *I've never had a love affair with life.* In the .38 he'd found it. I wondered if he thought beyond, thought to this moment and what it might do to me? I wondered if the hole that seemed to have opened in my soul would ever fill again.

"I'm sorry, Pete," Chief Romer said.

Nate was by my side by then. He'd heard enough to have a general idea of what was going on and was looking to me for some explanation.

"Ren filled in at the station sometimes. He gave me a ride home once or twice when the Scout let me sit," I said, as if that explained everything.

"Why the hell would he take my gun?"

Chief Romer shrugged. "Who can say? I've never yet been able to make sense of suicide. Why would a person with everything kill himself?"

"Maybe life was just too hard," I said.

"Too bad," Nate said. "That doesn't make it OK to steal my gun. And how . . . ?" He stopped, looked from me to the chief and back to me, then shook his head to himself.

Chief Romer sighed, scratched his head. "Like I said, suicide's a funny thing. Anyway, Pete, Nate, I'm sorry you had to be involved in all this. But since the gunshot was self-inflicted, once I've done all the paperwork, and satisfied his family's questions, I don't suppose there's any reason you can't have your gun back."

"Appreciate that," Nate said.

But I knew there was no way in hell that gun was ever coming back in my house.

That night, when I brought up the suit we'd never bought but still could if we just ran by the mall first thing in the morning, Nate said as busy as he'd been on the river he thought he'd probably just pass on the wedding. And in that moment, all of the anger and tension and questions that had been simmering in the weeks since he'd come home erupted.

Mostly when Nate and I had argued in the past, I did the yelling and Nate did the listening, and when he'd heard enough he left me to stew on my own. Normally, Nate retreated.

But this time, Nate yelled as loudly as I did. We covered everything: the suit and tie, me not being who I used to be, and who the fuck was this asshole who stole his gun?

"He wasn't an asshole. He was my friend." My voice quivered, and for a moment I thought maybe I would tell him the truth. Just get it out. Except, for what?

"Yeah well, your *friend* was a thief."

"Fuck you, Nate. I wish the hell you'd just stayed up on the slope."

"I know you do," he yelled back. And then, quietly, "Believe me, so do I."

He left then, calmly walked out the door and closed it behind him. I followed, opened the door, then slammed it myself.

ELEVEN

From the doorway of the old Russian Orthodox Church, I scanned the crowded pews. Skye waved from one near the front, and I let an usher guide me to the empty spot beside her. She wore Birkenstocks and a green gauzy skirt and top with matching ribbons in her hair.

"You're alone," she said.

I nodded. I didn't have it in me to explain. Nate had not come home the night before, or even called. I didn't know where he was or if he would ever be back, and I knew that was exactly what I deserved, but I was not going to let myself think about that just then. If he was gone, I would have the rest of my life to ponder what I had ruined.

"Me too," Skye said. "I always imagined Kyle and me here, our first wedding together."

"Have you heard from him lately?"

She shook her head. "Oh no. He disconnected his phone. Moved, no forwarding address."

"I'm sorry," I said.

"Me, too. I really cared for that guy, you know? I mean, how did everything get so . . . I don't know. I just remember all the good times back in the beginning. The sock hop, Valentine's. All right, maybe not all of Valentine's."

"Going to the chapel and we're gonna get married," I sang in a whisper.

"Yeah, those were the days. I always wonder about Di. If she ever got in touch with Denny. If she sees Billy. Is Denny OK?"

"I know. I wonder about it, too. I guess there's just some things we'll never know."

The church grew suddenly quiet. Up front, the former governor who was to perform the ceremony had taken his spot. The organist stopped. The fiddler drew his bow, and we all stood as Annie made her way up the aisle to her groom.

From the church we filed through town in a long procession of cars that someone had decorated with tissue flowers and streamers while we were inside. It was June, a notoriously dreary month, but the sun shone as bright as frigid December.

Annie's house sat on fifty acres with its own small lake. The yard out back had been set with folding tables and chairs, picnic tables, and a few Adirondacks and camp chairs, too. Tables overflowed with ice-filled trays of King Crab legs, smoked salmon, and oysters on the half shell. A pig roasted on a spit and several makeshift bars had been set up around the periphery of the yard, manned by the staff Annie had hired for the event.

Mitch worked the remote stereo equipment from a small booth that had been built to shelter him, and in the center of the lawn nearby was a portable parquet floor for dancing.

I walked across the lawn in the direction of some familiar faces. A radio squawked, and I saw the chief hurrying to turn down the volume on the radio clipped to his belt. I wagged a finger at him, and he grinned. "Good thing that didn't happen in the church, huh?" he said.

"You on duty, Chief?" I asked.

"I'm always on duty, Pete."

"Are you going to save me a dance?"

"Me?" He looked down at his shoes. "Two left feet."

"Save me one anyway."

I didn't realize it was Belinda behind the makeshift bar until she turned and fixed me with that glare.

"White wine, please," I said.

She stared a moment longer. "I know it was you with him that night. I know all about you two."

"You don't know a thing," I said. "Ren was my friend. That's it." It was the only thing I could say. I owed Nate that much. But I felt bad for her, too, and it seemed as much a kindness as a lie.

She looked at me, trying to decide what to believe. "Really, Belinda, he was just my friend." And I could see the moment when she decided to believe me, when the anger dissolved and there was nothing but grief.

She covered her face with her hands and took several deep breaths, then dropped her hands. "I knew he was going to do this. I knew it. I wanted so bad for him to . . . to just not die," she said.

"I'm so sorry."

She nodded. "He left some of his shirts at the laundry. You should come get one."

"Thanks," I said. "But that's OK. You go ahead and keep them."

She passed me my wine and I slipped an extra ten dollars in her tip jar.

And then there was Annie, grinning and looking like the perfect bride. She wore a floor-length ivory split skirt with a beaded and pearled halter top and matching cape, her hair French braided and sewn through with flowers and pearls.

"Hey sister, what do you think, not bad for an old broad who was never going to marry again, huh?" she said. We hugged.

"They'll be talking about this wedding for years," I said. "Everything's so beautiful."

"Thanks, hon. It is, isn't it. I forgot how much fun it is to be the bride. Hey, where's that handsome husband of yours?"

"Working, I guess," I said.

"I hear it's a banner year on the river," Annie said. "Fish are jumping, and the tourists are a-coming. The tavern has been crazy. I was thinking I'd close up for a week, but I don't dare now."

"Wait. What about your honeymoon?"

"Later. There's no time now. Jack's heading up north to glacier country to train with the dogs for the summer."

"He's leaving, Annie? So soon? You can't go with him?"

"You going to run the tavern for me, Pete? It's OK. He'll be back in the fall."

"But it's so soon, and you just married and everything. You remember what Denny said about absence making the heart go wander."

"And I don't believe it for a minute. Look at you, you did fine." And then, "Hey, Pete," she said, nudging me with an elbow, "look who's here." She pointed across the lawn.

He was talking to a man I recognized from the credit union, his sport coat slung over his shoulder, a new tie dangling from its pocket and his white shirt opened several buttons.

"Hey, Nathan, you handsome devil," Annie called to him. "You better save me a dance."

Nate turned toward us. He waved to her, then fixed me with a half smile, tipped his chin. Well? I started toward him, my high heels sinking into the ground with each step, until I stopped and slipped them from my feet and tiptoed across the grass.

"Jeff was just telling me about a Piper Cherokee they repossessed," Nate said, after he'd introduced us.

Jeff nodded. "Come by the office this week, Nate. Let's see what the numbers look like." Nate said he would, and Jeff headed for the keg. And there we were alone.

"You sitting anywhere?" he asked, finally.

"Not yet," I said.

Mitch said he was going to slow it down and cued up Eddie Rabbit and Crystal Gale's "Just You and I."

"Are you going to put your shoes on?" Nate asked.

"Hmmm?"

"You can't dance in flats, remember?" And for a second I saw a flicker of the old Nate, the Nate who loved to tease me.

We walked to the square of parquet. I reached for his arm for balance while I wiggled into my sandals, but it wasn't there. Then, seeing me, he offered it. The right thing to do. We were strangers again, this time without the warmth that comes with innocent expectation.

"Thanks," I said.

"New dress?"

"I never showed it to you?"

"Not me," he said.

I held up an edge of the handkerchief hem, so he could get the full view, the pink and white ribbons that edged the blue skirt and formed the spaghetti straps that tied at my shoulders.

"Very nice," he said.

"I got it on sale. I guess I should have said something."

"You earn your own money. You don't need my permission."

"That's not what I meant. I just like you to see what I buy. You're my partner."

"Oh yeah?"

We both sighed at the same time, and then smiled ruefully at our mutual unease. He scuffed at the grass with the toe of his loafer, then, seeing my glance, "Yeah, I know. I should have worn black shoes. I was going to go shopping, but my personal shopper wasn't available."

"You look good, Nate. Just right."

"Not like a hick?"

I felt the hopelessness of it then. I wasn't used to Nate's anger, and I wasn't up to it.

"Sorry," he said. "I'm an ass, I know."

"I had it coming."

"Come on," he said. He took my hand. I put the other on his shoulder, and slowly we made our way around the dance floor.

He sighed and breathed into my hair. "Ah, Blondie, I love you. I've always loved you."

"I'm so glad you're home, Nate. And I'm so sor—"

"Ssshh," he said. "Not today. Let's just be happy."

"Let's," I said.

"But, Pete?"

"Hmmm?"

"Who was this guy, anyway?"

I took a deep breath and thought for a moment. "I don't know. I really don't know." It was the truest thing I had. And I guessed I might look for the answer to that question for a hundred years and never find it. I didn't know anything. Only that I had liked him so much. So damned much.

Next to us, Skye danced with Terry. Annie and Jack had the center of the floor, and Harold waltzed Lydia Merit in a circle in the opposite corner. He caught my eye and winked. I winked back.

And in that moment, I knew things were just the way they were supposed to be. In any given second it could change, and it was a wise person who knew to appreciate the moment because you didn't get to go back and do it over again. All there was was what you had right then. There was no going back, no guarantees of going forward. Only the moment.

I scanned the crowd, people dancing, people talking, people balancing plates piled with the offerings of a feast the likes of which Wrassell might never see again. And then, there was Chief Romer walking our way, hand waving for my attention.

"Pete, you got yourself some sensible shoes around?" he asked, pulling the stir stick from his lips.

"These are my sensible shoes, Chief," I said.

"Better hurry up then. Looks like we've got a situation developing and it's big. Your competition's probably already on it."

"Sure, Chief," I said, thinking he was joking.

"Suit yourself," he said, then walked off. A few steps later, he turned back to me again, and waved an arm for me to follow.

"I think he's serious, Nate," I said.

"I think so, too, Blondie. Come on, I'll drive."

TWELVE

BREAKING NEWS, WRASSELL—BIDARKEE BAY, PETE NASH, KWLD—
Missing Couple Found.

A couple who vanished in March was found Saturday at the bottom of
a Bidarkee Bay lake in a vehicle originally reported as stolen.

Dianna Mack and Jeremy Smith, known locally on-air as Jeremy
Knight, were found by students in a diving class after they spotted the
Suburban on the lake bottom. Police believe the pair broke through
ice on the lake after taking the Suburban from an employee's home
the night they were last seen . . .

Robert Hansen was sentenced to a 461-year sentence in 1984 after pleading guilty to murdering four women. He confessed to authorities to killing seventeen women and raping thirty. Dubbed the Butcher Baker, Hansen was a pilot and owned a bakery in downtown Anchorage. He died at the age of seventy-five in an Anchorage hospital in August 2014.

BIOGRAPHICAL NOTE

Lori Tobias left her Pennsylvania hometown at eighteen for a brief visit with her Air Force–enlisted sister in Alaska. She stayed eight years, studying journalism at the University of Alaska and marrying her husband Chan in an A-frame church with a view of Denali. She has since lived in Connecticut, Washington, Southern Oregon, and Colorado. In her twenty-five years in journalism, she worked as a columnist and feature writer for the *Rocky Mountain News*, and covered the Oregon Coast as a staff writer for *The Oregonian*. She is a recipient of an Oregon Literary Fellowship. She currently lives on the Oregon Coast with her husband Chan and shelter rescue Mugsy.